WARNING

This book contains sexually explicit scenes and adult language. It may be considered offensive to some readers. This book is for sale to adults ONLY.

* * * * * * * * * * * * * * * * *

Please store your files wisely where they cannot be accessed by underage readers.

ISBN-13: 978-1988083872
ISBN-10: 1988083877

Other Books by Darla Dunbar:

<u>The Romeo Alpha BBW Paranormal Shifter Romance Series</u> (This series precedes the "<u>Romeo Alpha Blood Lines Romance Series</u>")

Amanda Walker thinks that she has a normal and boring life. That is until after her 24th birthday. Everything changes when she meets the man who says he was supposed to be her husband. Denying everything the man says, she fights him every step of the way. But after he kidnaps her, Amanda discovers that there are some things about her family that her parents kept a secret all these years. Among the history of the family she learns secrets she thought only happened in story books. Can Amanda tell the difference between truth and lies or is she this mysterious woman that holds the key to a legacy?

<u>The Alpha Feud BBW Paranormal Shifter Romance Series</u>

Eliza's life consisted of reporting on boring, crowd-pleasing events, like their country livestock fair. With the arrival of two handsome brothers, the lives of Eliza and her best friend, Melissa, are shaken to the core. For Eliza, the arrival of this new man becomes a test of her relationship with her current boyfriend, who she's been happily living with for over six years. Does Hayden, a complete stranger, really wield the power to make Eliza reconsider her relationship with Andrew?

The Alpha Packed BBW Paranormal Shifter Romance Series

Darlene has led a quiet life since suffering through a terrible break-up. She wants nothing more than to spend her time in front of the TV, away from any sort of trouble. But all that goes down the drain when handsome, rugged and rough Idris comes into her life. He is a werewolf on the lookout for his missing pack leader. Darlene quickly finds herself pulled towards this mysterious man and at the same time finds herself falling deeper and deeper into the world of the supernatural.

The Daemon Paranormal Romance Chronicles

The daemon infighting can only be stopped when a strong leader emerges to calm the different factions. Juno appears to be at the heart of the conflict. Things become complicated when Phoebe and Supay try to negotiate with the siren, Juno. The love triangle among Phoebe, Supay and Apollo become tense when Juno's meddling threatens to destroy any romance that develops.

The Mind Talker Paranormal Romance Series

Ananda finds herself on the run and she's not alone. With help from Jared, a stranger that she just met, the two evade capture by an organization that is intent on hunting her kind. Ananda and Jared are able to read minds. When an unfortunate incident happened involving a disturbed individual that resulted in the death of his schoolmates, the secret organization decided to take action.

This book is Part Two of the "Romeo Alpha Blood Lines Romance Series" and follows twenty-four years after "The Romeo Alpha BBW Paranormal Shifter Romance Series"

1 - Blood Lines

Twenty-four years have passed in relative peace for Amanda and Romeo. They've raised five children into adulthood and are thoroughly enjoying their lives as the Alpha King and Queen of the werewolves. At twenty-four, Sarina is just stepping into her powers and will be ripe for mating when her birthday comes in two weeks. What no one knows is the danger that lurks just outside their tight knit community. Romeo has made peace with the other clans and has enjoyed that peace, but it will all come crashing down around him when his oldest daughter comes of age to take a mate.

2 - Alpha Infiltration

Brody is an attentive and loving mate and Sarina finds herself engulfed by the love of her family. When things start to change with the twins though, Sarina finds herself torn in two. She loves Brody in a way she's never loved another man, human or wolf. When he shows signs of the dark void, however, she can't decide whether to run from him or to him. She's frightened for both of her sons and struggles with her own mortality.

3 - Alpha Bait

Lilith is on the loose, plotting and planning with Fenris to take down the Delta pack and its alpha, Romeo. Sarina and Brody have their work cut out for them in order to stop the hostile takeover. With their wedding on the horizon, both feel compelled to spend time with their family even as danger lurks around every corner. When the twin babies, Jedidiah and Brody Jr., go missing, all hands are on deck to search for the leaders of the next generation of the Delta pack. And as Sarina and Brody dig deeper into Lilith's past, especially where Romeo is concerned, they find a mind twisted by deception and an overly unhealthy obsession with power.

4 - Alpha Strategy

With Lilith's soul separated from her body, Romeo and Amanda are bent on seeing her body destroyed so that she never comes back again. What they've forgotten in the meantime is that Lilith wasn't alone in her desire over control of the Delta pack and Romeo. Sarina and Brody are finally enjoying a quiet life, not that they expect it to last long. Their wedding, a source of great stress, is just weeks away. With all that's going on though, Sarina wonders if she'll ever be able to legally wed her mate.

5 - Alpha Revelation

Lilith has haunted the Traverse family since the beginning but her obsession with the reigning alpha and his immediate family is more than Romeo's eldest daughter can stand. In a twisted allegiance with her first mate, Fenris, Lilith has caused unbearable pain to the Delta pack's community and now she has gone as far as to make a deal with the Devil. She has comfortably inhabited Sarina's body, playing wife to Brody and mother to the couple's twin boys. Digging her way up from Hell wasn't easy, but Sarina harnesses powers that rival even those of her mother.

Alpha Romeo Blood Lines Romance Series

Alpha Infiltration

Book Two

By Darla Dunbar

Copyright Revelry Publishing 2016

Table of Contents

Chapter One

"**YOU LOOK** awfully chipper this morning," Jason Traverse said to his twin when she strolled through the front door.

"Why shouldn't I be?" Sarina asked. She quirked an eyebrow at him as if to emphasize her point.

"Being pregnant, I'd think you'd be miserable," Jason smirked. "At least I sort of hoped you would be."

"Jerk," she said, teasing. Rounding the corner, Sarina greeted her mother, who was already up preparing breakfast.

"All grown up and still the bickering never stops," Amanda Walker-Traverse said, grinning at her daughter. "You do look lovely Sarina."

"At least someone in the family knows beauty when they see it."

"You get it from me, so it's only natural that I would," her mom said, laughing. "How's Brody?"

"Running around like a mad wolf. He seems to think these two will grow fast like Jason and I did."

"Well, werewolves do tend to grow much faster than their human counterparts," Amanda said, giving Sarina a gentle reminder.

"I know," she agreed. "I just don't think we need to baby proof the house today, or have a nursery ready yesterday. Brody insists on it so I just stay out of his way."

"I'm happy to know that he cares so much for you," Amanda said with a smile. "I have to admit there was a time, not so long ago, that we all worried that you'd made a mistake. Then, when you went through that period of forgetting when none of us knew who Brody was, it was just odd. Now that everything's back to normal, I can take a step back and tell you that you chose wisely. It was brash to say the least, but you knew your mate and never faltered from that decision."

"Thanks, Mama. Now if only Jason here could find himself a mate."

"Who says I haven't?" Jason said defensively. "I have a woman in mind. It just so happens not all of us are ready to jump on the matrimonial bandwagon as of yet."

"Oh please," Sarina scoffed. "I'll take my dying breath before you ever take a mate. You'd much rather just take a woman to your bed without all the trappings of a relationship. I know."

"I'm not denying that having a woman in my bed is nice, but lately I've come to realize that there's more to life than a couple of hours of passion in the night."

"Welcome to reality little brother," Sarina smiled.

"Can you two please talk about something other than sex at eight in the morning?" Amanda said.

Sarina took a seat close to her brother and thanked her mother for the French toast she'd been served. "This is amazing."

"You always say that," Amanda chuckled.

"That's because I'm always right," Sarina winked. "These two want more." She gestured to her belly.

"I was ravenous when I was carrying you two," Amanda said. Sarina watched her mother with a smile on her face. She'd taken her mother for granted, that much she knew. Still stunning at almost fifty in human years, Amanda was a picture of beauty. The way she moved showed strength and grace. Her hair still lustrous and dark as mahogany. Her eyes still sparkled when she smiled, which she did often, especially if the children's father was close by. "I'm surprised your father didn't kick me out when I got pregnant with Wade."

"Please," Sarina laughed. "Daddy's been crazy about you since day one. I've never seen any signs of that changing. If I didn't know better, I'd say you two are still on your honeymoon."

"We are darling," Amanda laughed. "Well, maybe not, but we're still over the moon about each other and we both know it. When you choose a mate there is no other who can turn your head."

"You're getting awfully sentimental on us in your old age, Mother," Jason teased. One look from her had him clearing his throat and stuffing his mouth with French toast.

"Careful now, pup," Romeo said with a grin as he entered the kitchen. "Old age or not, I'd still lay money on your mother to give you a good ass whoopin'."

"Yeah, yeah," Jason said with a wary smile.

Sarina loved these moments. It was one of the many things she'd miss now that she and Brody had finally finished moving everything into the home he'd been given when he'd conceded his leader status. Brody, Sarina's mate, had killed Reggie, the former alpha of his pack and taken over, all with the sensible intentions of bringing his pack under the tutelage and ruling right of Romeo and Amanda. As King and Queen of the Delta packs, it was only right that his pack join them. Since doing so, his pack had wanted for little and seemed even more settled than he'd ever seen them. Instead of living in caves like dogs, he was happy to report to Sarina and everyone else that his former pack was elated with how things turned out. They'd been given homes, food, necessities of everyday life and overall, they'd been well taken care of.

Brody, in exchange for his submission, had been given prominent status within the pack as a general. He helped Romeo keep the pack together and content, working as a liaison for those who lived further away from New Delta, making sure everyone had the necessities they needed. For her part, Sarina was happy to be pampered as her unborn twins continued to grow strong and rather quickly. She wasn't sure they were developing as fast as she and Jason had, but she was already showing and they'd only found out about the babies a month ago. At the rate she was going, it'd be well under half of the normal human pregnancy term when she would be ready to deliver. No wonder werewolves multiplied so quickly.

Finding her mother after breakfast, Sarina voiced her concerns. "I'm thinking about asking Brody if we should stay near the hospital from April on until the babies arrive."

"That's not a bad idea, although having them at home isn't a bad option either. I learned a lot about myself when I was having you. I found a confidence and reliance on myself and the ones I love. I probably wouldn't have noticed had I not been able to deliver you as I did."

"It's scary this first time."

"It's always a little bit of an anxious time, although I will say the first time there is always the unknown. I will support you in whatever you decide, Sarina."

"I'll see what Brody says and let you know from there."

"You do that, sweetheart. Meanwhile, I've got some major craft projects to get started if we're going to have these babies taken care of when the time comes. Never let anyone tell you twins don't run in families."

Fenris sat back and contemplated his next move. Sending the young buck, Brandt, to seduce and impregnate Romeo's eldest had been a stroke of genius on his part. Now to wait and see if the seed she carried belong to Brandt or her worthless wolf of a mate. Fenris was already smiling, just thinking about it. It wouldn't truly matter of course. He'd rip them apart no matter whose seed she carried.

He'd thought long and hard over the last several weeks about how to go about his first strike. He wanted it to hurt… a lot. Romeo needed to know and understand that he was not the alpha in charge. It wouldn't be easy, as taking down any alpha never was, but Fenris knew that given the alternative, Romeo would bow his knee to him.

He could almost see that moment and could admit that it turned him on. Having the play of any female he wished, including Romeo's sweet wife, or even one of his succulent daughters. Brandt had howled for days about the one called Sarina and how beautiful she was. Fenris couldn't blame him for getting hooked on her. An alpha's daughter was no small prize and if she was beautiful and put out as hotly as Brandt proclaimed, Fenris himself might even give her some enviable attention.

At any rate, Fenris knew that his first strike had to be the hardest and most elusive. If he did it right, and he damn well would, Romeo Traverse and his family would have no choice but to submit to his ruling. The thought of ruling the entire Delta area sent a ripple of fire through his blood as he thought about making the Traverse family pay. They'd been a thorn in his side ever since they'd split from his line. Now he'd finally worked out a plan that would set things right. He could hardly wait to get started.

"Dankar!" Fenris shouted. His patience, he could admit, wore thin during times when he was thinking about what was coming.

"You called for me sir?"

"I need you to do whatever it is you did to Brandt again. It needs to be perfect and if you can manage a longer time, that'd be in your best interest as well."

"I'll get right on it, sir."

"See that you do."

<<◇>>

Brandt met Dankar in his quarters. "You wanted to see me, Dankar?"

"Yes, yes," the small man said. "Come, sit."

Brandt did as he was bade and sat in the chair where Dankar had worked on him the last time. "I presume that Fenris wanted you to make me like Brody again?"

"Yes," Dankar replied, his tone short.

"Remember, Dankar, you may be Fenris' right hand man, but it is I who watches your back. Show some damn respect."

"Yes, Brandt," said Danker, but guardedly this time.

Brandt watched the little man mix potions and concoctions of who-knew-what brew. The noxious fumes were almost enough to make him pass out. He hoped that whatever it was that Dankar was doing, that it worked well and fast, because the last thing he wanted was to have to drink some nasty shit.

"This may not feel nice," Dankar said to him as he injected him with a large dose of some neon fluid. "But it should let you have an uninterrupted two weeks with Sarina and her family. Don't screw it up"

Brandt went back to his room and awaited the change he knew was coming. The first time had been less than pleasant as his body shifted into that of the alpha's daughter's mate. He'd had twenty-four hours last time. If he had to account for fourteen days, this was going to royally suck. Like most synthetic drugs it took nearly twenty minutes to feel the effects, but once they started, Brandt could hardly breathe. Even going from man to wolf, his change always started in his eyes.

Pain shot through his irises and into his optic nerves as brown turned to blue and his pupils dilated. With his pupils the size of dimes, he was thankful his room had no windows. The light he had forgotten to shut off streamed into his vision, making Brandt curse as he swiped a hand down the wall, desperately trying to find the switch. "Shit!" he growled as his body, relentless under the pressure of the drug's interference, continued its change. His shoulders widened and his torso and legs lengthened. The muscles in his arms, thighs and abdomen stretched and added new tissue as his body grew from a modest five foot eleven, to the taller Brody, who easily stood six foot, three inches. His jaw cracked and widened, giving him the strong jawline Brody sported. The hair on his head grew thicker, sprouting thousands of new hairs to add the lush texture of Brody's dark locks.

Two hours after it had all begun, Brandt was finally able to look in the mirror and see Brody standing there. His eyes, now crystal blue, smiled when he did. The facial hair, dark in texture and color, much like his hair, was easy to shave. He knew from watching, that Brody rarely wore a beard or let his facial hair grow much past a five o'clock shadow. He scowled, smiled, frowned and made every facial expression he could think of to make sure the process had changed his physical appearance in every way.

"It looks as if all went well," Dankar said, standing in Brandt's doorway.

"Screw you," Brandt said, glaring at Dankar. "The only solace I have is that I have two weeks to forget the pain. I may want to kill you when I change back. Be mindful to keep your distance from me when I do."

"I won't forget," Dankar said. Brandt could have sworn a grin crossed the man's face. If he didn't know better, he'd lay money on the pain being the most enjoyable part for Dankar when he concocted his potions. He had yet to use one that didn't have some sort of pain with it.

Chapter Two

Sarina spent the afternoon visiting members of the pack who were further out from town and rarely made it to meetings and such. She always carried copies of notes she made so that they would know how things were going peace-wise and would feel more connected to the main group. She'd just left the Rietger's home and was heading toward the Schultz's when she spotted Brody heading towards her. She could have sworn he'd been in more formal clothes when she'd left her parent's home. Now, though, he was more relaxed in a pair of jeans and a t-shirt. She smiled, thinking that no matter what he wore, he was sexy as hell.

"Hello, handsome," she smiled.

"Hey yourself, gorgeous." He grinned, but pulled her close when she got within arm's length. His mouth fused hotly to hers and their tongues tangled as his hands roamed up her side to cup her breast.

"Easy," she giggled. "We're in public. Not to mention I still get nauseous."

"Right," he sighed. "How's it going?"

"They seem happy, well taken care of. I never understood why my dad let everyone spread out as they chose. After seeing them today though, I understand it was because he knew the needs of his pack. He knew that not everyone wanted to be in town, so he let them choose where they wanted to be and committed himself to keeping them in the pack. Not just any alpha can do that.”

“No,” he agreed. “There are those of us who are willing to put ourselves on the line for those we care for.”

“Don’t be jealous,” Sarina smiled. “I love you just as fiercely as I love my extended family.”

“Want to go home and finish what I started out here on the street?”

“Yes,” she said, not blushing. Sarina had learned so much about herself since finding Brody. She was much more confident in her skin than she’d have thought, and their sex life was still extremely active, even though she appeared to be nearly five months pregnant in human terms. The fact that she was actually only about ten weeks along in real time made no difference. In a little over six weeks, her babies would be here and her family would grow exponentially. “However, I still have three homes to stop by before I can head home. I’ll be there before you know it though. Maybe we can get a nightcap before I crash.”

“Sounds good, baby.”

“I love you, Brody.”

"Love you, too," he said, smiling before he brought her close for another kiss.

Sarina watched Brody turn and head back toward town. He'd had an edge to him today, one she hadn't noticed since they'd made love in the shower. Something about him was harder and needier than he usually showed her, especially now that she was expecting. Lately she was the one who'd been initiating anything physical between them. She wasn't complaining… it was just nicely odd to see Brody's want for her, to know that even as her body changed to accommodate their babies, he still found her attractive and desirable.

She finished with the three families she'd promised to visit that day and headed home, anticipation revving in her system as she neared. She'd been impressed with Brody when he'd taken to caring for the home. Brody had been given a nice three bedroom, two bath home on the edge of town, close to her parents. It was close enough for Sarina to feel the warm comfort of her parents and siblings, but far enough away that a call was necessary before anyone visited. Thankfully her relatives were nice enough to understand their need for space as the babies grew closer to being delivered. She had plenty of girl time with her mother and sister, Shawna, and Aunt Penelope, but sometimes she wanted nothing more than to spend a quiet night at home with Brody, just the two of them. The babies, she knew, would be there before either of them was truly ready and times like tonight would be rare. She wanted to squeeze every bit from just the two of them before her time came to transition into motherhood.

"Honey, I'm home," she chuckled. She washed her hands at the kitchen sink and lifted the lid on the teriyaki chicken she was slow cooking before she headed upstairs to find her man. She knew tonight was the full moon and although she was thankful to exclude herself from the change, she still wanted to be there, as she always was, to watch Brody transition.

"Hey baby," Brody said when she entered their room. "I missed you today."

"Seeing me this afternoon wasn't enough, huh?"

"What?" Brody asked. Sarina watched him pick through the closet, trying to find something to wear that he wouldn't mind getting shredded tonight. "I didn't see you this afternoon."

"You don't remember stopping me out by the Schultz's and kissing me brainless?"

"Hon, I'd damn well remember if my lips had touched yours this afternoon," Brody smiled. Turning he came toward her in a way that always made Sarina's belly jump. She'd never met a man who could master the prowler stance as fluidly in his male form as he did in his wolf form, until Brody that is. The man exuded confidence as if he was born with a natural well of it inside himself. It was a major turn-on for her.

"I'm telling you, babe. You were wearing jeans and a t-shirt and your hair was all messy. Then you pulled me close and kissed me as if I was your last breath. Hot as hell if you ask me."

"Sorry I missed it," Brody grinned. "But I'm telling you doll, that I was with your dad up until about an hour and a half ago, well past the time you're saying you saw me. Not that I'm not obliged now to make it up to you. I don't want you getting disappointed and letting strange men take liberties with you."

"Liberties," Sarina laughed. Blowing it off as an odd misunderstanding, Sarina giddily met Brody's warm smile with her own. She could admit that she missed the fiery passion that had flowed between them so easily in those first months. She glimpsed it once in a while, when Brody's hands bruised her flesh in the heat of orgasm, or when the hickeys he left on her skin took a bit longer to heal, but it did little to satiate the need she had for him. Making love as often as they did, did little to stem the want he drew up in her. Still, she knew someday when the babies had grown up a bit, they'd get back to the moon-howling sex they'd enjoyed. She knew from talking with her mother candidly about it that the passion was easily put aside when babies were little and needy.

"As they grow and become more independent though, you and Brody will rekindle that fierce need for each other. I've been with your father for twenty-five years and we show little sign of slowing down, especially since we won't be having any more babies."

"Do you miss it?" Sarina had asked her mother then.

"No," she smiled. "Time moves on and so does a parent's role in their child's life. I'm no longer the mother who needs to chase you around, to discipline and teach you. Now, as a friend, I can sit back and love the woman you've become, help you through this stage in life and be there to love the babies you carry. If anything, I'm greatly looking forward to this time."

"Good," Sarina laughed. "Because if our passion comes back too strong, I may be calling you to babysit."

"I'd love to," Amanda had agreed. "Once a week, but no more. I can't keep my own passion bottled up if I take on little ones more often than that."

"I'll tell Brody to put a lid on it if he gets too frisky before date night."

"You'd better." Amanda laughed.

"Your mind is wandering again," Brody said gently. Sarina felt him nibble on her neck and laid her hand on the back of his head, threading her fingers through the thick hair he let grow long and shaggy most of the time.

"Sorry," she smiled. "Kiss me so I can stop thinking."

Brody did as she asked, falling easily into her and the heat they created together. His lips roamed over her face, jaw and neck, enjoying the way her breathing picked up as his hands worked her body over. They had to learn to slow down, to truly enjoy this process as Sarina grew heavier with their children. Now, Brody found that while he sometimes missed that instant flash and burn of passion they'd had in the very beginning, there was a sweetness here they would have easily missed if not for the twins. "The babies are quiet tonight."

"Just wait," Sarina chuckled. "Make me come and they won't be."

"Really?"

"It seems to be like a shot of adrenaline to them. They bounce all over the place in there after we have sex."

"I might have to do this with you more often. I do want athletic and active children after all."

"Our kind isn't active enough?" she asked. Then she quirked that dark eyebrow up in the way he loved and Brody was reminded all over again just why he loved her.

"Just in case," Brody smiled. She came to him easily then, her lips meeting his. Her tongue slid hungrily into his mouth, jacking his own need up a notch. Using his hands now, Brody showed her the need she easily pushed into him. He cupped her breasts, kneading them so their tips peaked for his pleasure. He drew her shirt aside, reveling in the beauty of her gorgeous breasts. She'd been blessed with perky breasts and now they were even more rounded as they prepared for the two lives she carried. Just the thought of her having his babies was a turn-on, even if it had been an unexpected one.

Taking her hands, Brody led Sarina to their bed, letting her sit down. He removed her shoes and the stockings she'd worn under her skirt that emphasized her incredible ass. He appreciated that she took time for herself, to keep herself healthy. Frankly he didn't care if anyone else thought so, but Brody found Sarina to be the most phenomenal-looking woman, or wolf come to think of it, that he'd ever laid eyes on. He gave some leeway because they were mates, but very little. "You need more rest," he said, noticing the swelling in her feet.

"Considering how fast this pregnancy is progressing, I would be surprised if my feet weren't swollen all day, every day. Swelling at night is normal, as long as it's just my feet. Aren't there other parts of my body that need to swell a little?"

"You're a bit frisky tonight," Brody chuckled.

"Seeing you this afternoon turned me on. Am I to be punished for enjoying the way my mate touches me?"

"No," Brody grinned. "Not unless punishment includes moaning when I fill you."

"Bring it on baby," she smiled.

Laying her back, Brody stripped her slowly, planting hot kisses and tongue trails along her skin. He started at her ankles and kissed his way up her thighs, making her moan when his fingers found her unbelievably hot pussy. He fingered her purposefully as his cool tongue circled her hyper-sensitive clit. He felt her body clench as she started to move against him. Her body, still lithe despite her growing belly, trembled as his hands took her over that first time. Moving quickly now, with Sarina's help, Brody stripped his own clothes off and lay down next to Sarina, letting his hand caress her. He ran circles over her nipples and then bent to taste them with his tongue, enjoying the way she sighed. He suckled one while his hand massaged the other. Then he alternated his attention as he rose over her, settling himself gently between her hips. When her belly proved to be a hindrance to that particular position, however, Brody helped her onto her hands and knees. Brody particularly liked the look of Sarina when he was taking her from behind. He was sure it had to do with the alpha in his blood, the submissive pose of her body, but whatever it was, it was one hell of a turn-on.

He rubbed her naked bottom, smacking a hand down across her ass and grinning when he heard her cuss, right after moaning. He knew she enjoyed the painful pleasure as much as he did. He was cautious now though to keep it to a minimum, afraid that it might harm the babies. He rubbed the red welt on her ass cheek as he positioned himself behind her, his tip feeling the ripe wetness of her folds. "I miss taking you hard and fast," he said, right before he filled her fully. Her moan made it hard to control the man, let alone the wolf who would have his time tonight.

She moaned again and again as he filled her, pulling out fully and filling her just the same. The long, full strokes provided little reprieve for the animal that yearned to mate the way they had in the beginning. Brody grabbed a fistful of Sarina's long hair, giving a tug that had her head snapping back as she moaned. "God, Sarina. Take me, baby. I want you so damn bad right now."

"Brody," she cried as her body exploded. He felt the jerking of her completion as her body trembled under his hands. Locking her hips in his hands, Brody gave two hard thrusts and spent himself into her heated center. Pulling back, Brody managed to fall off the bed before the change took him over.

Chapter Three

Brandt sat outside Brody and Sarina's home, waiting. The wolf in him knew that tonight they'd change, although the moon hadn't quite risen yet. Still, he had ears to hear and the sounds coming from their house left little to be imagined. He was edgy tonight, knowing how badly he wanted to get his own hands on Romeo's daughter made it difficult to know that her mate was the one taking her. He wondered how they'd made it around the conversation they'd surely had. Brody must have been one confused bastard when Sarina mentioned seeing him that afternoon.

Brandt knew from experiencing her that she liked it hard and rough just as much as gentle and drawn out. Maybe she'd decide to keep them both. Brody could give her the loving, caring mate she wanted and he'd gladly wait around to take her six ways to Sunday when she had the mind to get good and screwed. Just thinking about it was making his jeans uncomfortable. As the full moon rose higher in the sky, Brandt felt himself shift into the wolf, howling when his animal was finally free. Tonight he'd feast, but the wolf in him wanted something a little hotter than prey right at the moment.

Leaping into the woods, Brandt lifted his large head and sniffed the air. The Delta had to have some female wolves who were single and in heat. Not every female found her mate as quickly as Sarina had. He moved along an old path that led deeper into the woods, coming close to a cabin that had its lights on. His nose picked up a hot scent and Brandt followed it around the cabin until he saw the silhouette of a wolf beside the cabin. Watching, Brandt sat on his hind legs to wait. A buck kicked wildly in the air briefly before he saw the wolf rip its throat out. Giving a whine of request, Brandt was pleasantly surprised when the wolf dragged the buck's limp body over and dropped it at his feet. He sniffed the beautiful female wolf who'd shared her bounty. She was definitely a breeder and in season if he wasn't mistaken. The blood of a wolf was pungent in a way human blood wasn't. Nipping at her neck, Brandt felt his loins burn as she bowed to him, rolling on her back to expose the tender flesh of her underbelly to him. A classic sign of submission, the female, whoever she was, offered more than her meal to him. Playfully, Brandt encouraged her until she stuck her ass in his face, a blatant invitation. He took her, before she could back out.

Mounting her, Brandt used his teeth to hold her as he entered her. The first stroke was easy, feeling the depth of her body. As he pulled out though, Sarina's body, the way she'd given herself to him pulsed through his memory. Taking the wolf underneath him, Brandt took her thrust after ruthless thrust, the ache in his body a need he couldn't control. He barely heard the female wolf whimper as he had his way with her over and over again. His orgasm left him physically spent so that he had to lie down to eat the carcass the female had brought out. He felt bad when she too lay down, her body obviously wrecked by him. He had no doubt that she'd be good and bruised when sunup came, but he couldn't take it back now.

Sitting up, he touched his nose to hers, whining at her until she started to eat. He wanted her to know that he appreciated her offer and the time they'd shared. She'd been sacrificial and he wouldn't forget it. He'd even entertain the idea of mating with her if she could put out like that as a human also. Her pussy, despite being in her wolf form, had been hot and ripe. Brandt wouldn't forget it and stayed with her through the night.

Morning came and Brandt woke to see the woman lying naked in the grass, her body shivering after the morning dew had settled. Her neck sported four shallow holes where his teeth had pierced her and her hips and bottom showed some serious bruising. Bending down, Brandt picked her up and took her into the cabin. He put her gently in the bed and covered her body with the thick comforter. Pushing her light hair back he saw a beautiful face, her brow furrowed as she continued to shiver. "Are you alright?" he asked, his voice rusty and rough from sleep.

She turned and bright green eyes met his. "No one's ever touched me with that sort of need," she sighed. "I've been through more wolves than I care to remember and no one's ever needed me like that."

"Why have you been passed along?"

"It would seem that I cannot breed. What good is a wolf that can't carry life? I'm no more than a harlot among my pack. They use me at their will. That's why I hunt alone. I was afraid that if I refused you, you'd force me."

"I've never forced anyone," Brandt said, thankful, especially now that he spoke the truth. "Would you consider being with a wolf that wasn't interested in breeding?"

"You don't want to breed?"

"No," he said. "I want to be free to be myself as a human or a wolf. Having to take care of pups doesn't fit that want very well."

"I'm not sure I can keep up with you," she smiled. "One time and my body is wrecked."

"My needs aren't always so fierce," he said, hoping she'd agree. Having a woman or wolf at his disposal when he wanted a good lay was something he'd needed for a while. "I'd be good to you."

"I'll need to wait a while, heal a bit before we make love again."

"I'm not sure we could call what happened last night making love. It was definitely mating, just without the bites to seal the deal."

"True," she grinned. Brandt sighed. He'd found a woman who couldn't breed, who was both beautiful and willing. A wolf and man who didn't want children could hardly ask for more.

"I'll come back and check on you tonight," Brandt said. He foraged in the cupboards and found some food for her. He also grabbed her a bottle of water before he pressed a kiss to her brow and left to do some reconnaissance.

<<◇>>

Sarina woke the next morning to see Brody lying next to her. She didn't know when he'd gotten in and assumed that it was after sunrise as he was clothed. The first time she'd skipped the change, he'd gotten in so late that he'd been naked under the covers. She had gladly taken advantage of the situation and had woken him with a long session of sexual bliss. Lately though she knew he dressed so she wouldn't wear herself out. Little did he know just how much waking to him in the morning turned her on. Still, she let him sleep and tiptoed to the shower.

She dressed easily, thankful for the maternity clothes her mother had given her. She ate well, before leaving a note for Brody and heading out to see her mother. She needed to see about getting the Radiants together. She knew the risks of joining their powers in close quarters, but Sarina needed some advice because things were picking up quicker and quicker with the twins and she wanted to be prepared for all possible outcomes.

<<◇>>

"You look well rested," Amanda said as she worked in her garden.

"I am. It's nice to take a break from the change. I know it won't last, but I'm enjoying it while it does."

"I agree," Amanda smiled. "So, tell me what's on your mind."

"Am I that easy to read?"

"You are to your mother," said Amanda.

Sarina looked at her mother then and realized just how blessed she was. Amanda had gone from being a normal, non-suspecting woman to finding out about her parentage, a combination of werewolf and witch, practically overnight. And she'd still managed to rise above it all to become the reigning Queen of the Delta pack. Sarina's parents were the solid foundation she'd relied on since birth and there was no way to express how much she still needed them.

"I'm nervous," Sarina finally said. "I'm not sure I'm ready for all of this."

"By all of this I assume you mean the twins?"

"That and all the changes having children bring. Brody and I are still settling down. In a couple of months we'll be responsible for two beautiful babies."

"I remember feeling just like that when I realized you and Jason were coming. I was even more scared because your father had been captured by Dean and Damon was nowhere to be found. I felt like I had no one to rely on. Then your Aunt Audri and Alessandra and Catrona, two of the original Radiants, showed up to rescue me. Aunt Penelope was there as well, which made me feel horrible."

"Why?"

"Because while I was over the moon crazy about your dad, she wasn't free to love your uncle as she wished. She and Elijah had spent years trying to ignore the way they felt about each other, only to be denied their happily-ever-after because of the gift she had. When both Alessandra and Catrona died and passed their powers on to their daughters, they all decided that I should lead the Radiants. That's when I made the change to the way we operate. It is one of the few things I know I did right back then. I still remember how wonderful it was to be a witness to the love those two shared. Sweetheart, you and Brody will screw up and make plenty of mistakes. No parent gets through raising their children any other way. However, if you work to love each other, love your children with everything you are, and provide them with stability, a loving dose of discipline when they need it, and a healthy dose of fun filled memories, you'll do just fine."

"I'm glad someone thinks so," Sarina sighed. "I know that it's a taboo subject, but I need to know what you think of inviting Aunt Briana and Aunt Lucia here for a baby shower."

"You want all of the Radiants to get together in this small of a space? Don't you remember what I told you last time?"

"I know," Sarina rushed on. "I know that having them stay is out of the question. I just thought it'd be nice to see you all together, and I need a little reassurance from the powers that be."

"Alright, sweetie. I'll give them a call and see what they say. It may take a week or two, but we'll see if we can't get you an overnight visit."

"Thanks, Mama."

"You're welcome, honey."

Sarina stepped out the door of her parent's home, the home that had once belonged to her great Aunt Mabel, with a spring in her step. She was going to get the answers she was looking for concerning the twins and just maybe some insight into the dreams she'd been having lately.

"Hey, sexy mama," Brody said, looking very proud of himself.

"Hey, handsome." Sarina smiled. "What are you doing here? You're supposed to be out with Dad."

"I took off early," Brody said, pulling her close to nuzzle her neck. "After last night I can't seem to think about anything else except having you again."

"You're awfully frisky lately. I'm not complaining. It's just an observation."

"Does that mean you want to skip lunch and have a little dessert first?"

"With these two still in here? I don't skip anything anymore."

"Oh fine, we'll feed you. Then we'll enjoy dessert."

"Sounds good to me," she agreed.

<<◇>>

Brandt smiled as he walked Sarina home. His plan was going rather smoothly all things considered. He still had to tie up the loose end in the cabin, but right now all his body wanted was to satiate his need with the woman on his arm.

"You've been acting awfully odd lately," said Sarina.

"Have I?"

"Last night when I mentioned seeing you earlier in the afternoon you acted as if I was out of my mind. You still don't remember?"

"Of course I remember," said Brandt, smiling. "How could I forget kissing you brainless? I'm not sure we've kissed like that in a while. I can do more kissing like that, you know."

"Easy, tiger. Let the pregnant woman eat. I'll need the calories to keep up with you."

"How about we pick something up and head out into the woods?" asked Brandt.

"You want to picnic?"

"It is how we first started isn't it?"

"Yes," Sarina said with a grin. Flashbacks to her first encounters with Brody sprang to her mind. They'd been so uncontrollable back then. Not that it had really been that long ago. Six months together was nothing compared to some people, her parents, for example.

"It never hurts to get back to our roots," he said.

"Alright," she agreed.

They picked up sandwiches, chips and two bottles of water before Brandt led her into the woods where a thick patch of grass grew in the sunshine. "I've always loved this spot," he said, opening her door.

"Me too," she blushed. "Especially after being here with you." They ate, talking about the twins and how things were going with her dad.

"Things are great. My pack seems truly happy for the first time in a long, long time. Your dad is a great leader."

"I'm glad you think so. It took a lot of guts to submit your pack and place to him like you did. I think it really showed how much you loved me as well."

"I hope so," Brandt said. It was so much easier than he'd originally thought. Vulnerable and gullible. Sarina was one easily seducible woman.

Chapter Four

Sarina finished off her sandwich, burped, blushed and said, "Excuse me."

"Good food always deserves a belch," Brandt said. "At least that's what my mother used to say."

"She must have been a smart woman."

"She was," he smiled. "She would have loved you. And the twins… don't even get me started."

"Actually, getting you started is half of the reasons we're out here right now."

Crawling on her hands and knees, she pressed her body against him, liking the way he just lay back for her.

"I guess we've moved onto dessert now," said Brandt.

"Not even close, baby."

"Well then," he grinned. "Let me assist you."

Need, the edgy sort that made for jerky, hurried movements, pumped through Sarina as she hurriedly stripped her clothes. Her breasts ached as Brandt's mouth found her tight nipples. That only fueled her hot pussy. The last time she'd felt this insanity was when they'd screwed in the shower five and a half months earlier. She didn't mind the gentle and easy slowness of most of their encounters now, but there was something wonderful to be said for the heated, crazy passion of sex that drove her to the edge of her sanity.

They made love, or screwed rather, before Brandt finally set in motion the events that would seal his status among his pack. He'd have everyone, including Fenris, wondering if the alpha status would change hands. Then he'd move to the cabin and have his way with the beauty who was recovering from the last time he'd had her.

Taking out a rope from his pocket, he took Sarina's hand and tied it around her wrist.

"You're seriously going to tie me up? I've had this fantasy a time or two, but never like this. I'm not sure I can do another round at this rate," said Sarina.

"I'm not just tying you up, darling. I'm kidnapping you."

"Brody," Sarina said, laughing. "You're an idiot. I love you, but you're so dense sometimes."

"I wouldn't be the dense one, sweetheart. I'm not Brody. My name is actually Brandt Medford. I only look like your mate. Thanks in large part to the black magic used in my pack. I will say though that I really enjoyed having my way with you again. The first time, in the shower at your parent's house, was rather phenomenal."

He could see the realization setting in and stood back as she retched on the ground. All things considered, he couldn't exactly blame her. "You were the one who met me yesterday. That's why Brody didn't know what I was talking about. Tell me what you want."

"Not so much me, per se. My alpha, Fenris, really, really wants your daddy-o to acquiesce and turn over the Delta pack. That being said, we both know that won't ever happen, unless the risk equals the reward. Your dad loves you, more so than your siblings, although snagging any of you probably would have worked. However, thanks to my hook-up, snatching you was almost too easy."

"Why would you do this?"

"Initially, I needed the recognition. Fenris just wanted to start a war. I made him see the wisdom in getting some inside intel on your pack. I couldn't just go to your dad and ask how things were. So, I waited it out and did my research covertly. I couldn't pass up the opportunity to have you though. Christ, you were ripe. All in season and ready to mate. I wonder if the babies in your womb are mine or his. Maybe you'll get super lucky and have one baby from both of us, eh?"

Sarina wanted to vomit. What sick son-of-bitch did something this insane? "So you tried to impregnate me just because you wanted to have sex? Are the females in your pack that low that you had to come looking elsewhere?"

"No, although the women in my pack have nothing on an alpha's daughter. You are so very nice. Actually though, I did it as a way to force your father's hand. If even one of those little rats is mine, you'll forever be subject to the rules of my pack. I will own you, at least partially. Your father will gladly submit to freeing you from that parental contract and Fenris will be able to make the Delta pack all his."

"You're an idiot," Sarina sneered. "My father will never bow to your leader. I don't give a damn if he is the Fenris who started our line or not. You can do whatever you like to me but my father will continue to rule."

"Whatever you say, darling. Right now all I care about is getting you nice and comfortable. I have some things to see to."

Sarina tried to stay calm, even more aware of her condition now that she was no longer in control of her surroundings. She tried to remember which way they'd gone. Looking at trees and such as they passed them didn't help in the least. "I can walk, please."

"Don't make me regret being nice to you," he said. Sarina looked into eyes that looked so much like Brody's. It broke her heart that she hadn't seen past his mask. The fact that she'd slept with him, twice now, that he could be the father of her twins made her heart hurt. Would Brody forgive her? Would he understand that she hadn't known? Deciding she needed to leave a marker, Sarina bit the ends of her hair off and tossed them down. She knew it was risky as they'd be virtually invisible to anyone looking through human eyes. Still, she had to hold onto hope that once Brody and her family knew she was missing, they'd do what was necessary to find her again.

"We're here," Brandt said. Sarina stood stock still as people stared. "Everyone, this is Sarina Traverse, the Delta alpha's daughter. As you can see, she'd in a delicate state so we need to make sure she's comfortable and cared for. Men, keep your distance. The females will tend to her, and only the females."

Sarina felt like a piece of meat at the market. Everyone seemed to look her over as if to ask themselves if she was worth the price. She damn well was. She was a damn Traverse after all. "I need something to drink."

"We have bourbon," one young woman said, her bright blue eyes hopeful.

"I can't have alcohol, sweetie."

"How about some water, or juice? We have plenty of both."

"Water would be wonderful."

She was fed and given water before Brandt showed her to his chambers.

"I won't sleep in the same room with you," said Sarina defiantly.

"You'll do as I say if you want to see those babies born," he said, his face so full of anger that Sarina hoped Brody was never that mad at her. She had the urge to spit in his face but knew it'd end badly. With the twins so close to delivering, she couldn't risk them just for her own gratification.

Brody headed home after a long day with Romeo. His body ached, but there was a part of him that yearned for his wife. He knew her time was close with every passing day. Still, it was nearly impossible, once he wanted her, to deny either of them the pleasure. He'd been surprised to find a tender side to love making. He'd always only had it hot and heavy. Then Sarina had told him they were expecting and everything had changed. He'd watched her go from a beautiful young woman, who happened to be in her first season, to a gorgeously stunning mother and the change had affected him profoundly. He wanted her happiness in a way he hadn't known before. He wanted to give her every opportunity to smile and enjoy their lives together. He knew when her time came, it'd be hard to watch her labor and give birth. He knew it wouldn't be easy to see her suffering, but still the idea of becoming a father to not one, but two babies… that was thrilling.

"Hey babe!" he called when he stepped through the door. He sat his jacket down and took the items he carried to the counter in the kitchen. He noticed she'd made peach cobbler and helped himself to a bite. Figuring she was probably napping, Brody snuck upstairs. Opening their bedroom door he looked around the room, confused. The shower wasn't running, but he checked the bathroom just in case. Even after a quick check of the basement, he told himself he was being irrational. Still, he called Romeo and Amanda to see if she happened to be there.

"She left this afternoon after stopping by for a visit," Amanda said. "You're sure she's not there?"

"No," he said, his voice concerned. "I've checked the bathroom, our bedroom, even the basement. She's nowhere to be seen here."

"Come here, Brody," Romeo ordered. "We'll organize a search party."

Brody met Sarina's parents outside their home. "Tell me anything you know that seemed odd to you. Anything, even the slightest clue might help."

"Yesterday we were getting ready for bed. I knew the change was coming and I wanted her comfortable before it happened so I wouldn't have to worry about her afterward. She said something about seeing me yesterday afternoon while she was out visiting the Schultz's and such. She said I kissed her senseless, except I never saw her yesterday afternoon. We were just—"

"I need everyone, Amanda. Everyone who can get here within the next half an hour," Romeo ordered, thankful he didn't need to tell her twice to make the calls. "I think we've been infiltrated. Lilith, Fenris' lover did this to us a while back, before you and Sarina met. She pretended to be an idiot the entire time, for years possibly. All just to get close to me. She had some delusion about being with me and ruling the Delta pack. If we've been infiltrated, it's possible that Fenris' other line is behind this."

"You're saying that there's someone out there who looks like me?"

"It's possible. Black magic is very potent and powerful stuff. It's nothing to be trifled with, I know that. If Fenris' other line wants a war, they've chosen a wise first move. It gets me to come to them, ask for her back. I'm sure they'll demand submission from me and when I refuse they'll hurt her. If only she could tap into the powers she gained from her mother."

"She can't turn," Brody said adamantly.

"No and she won't. She's too close to delivering to do much of anything, but if I know Amanda, she'd already be working on a locator spell."

"I made the calls. Everyone who can come will be here in less than thirty minutes. In the meantime I'm going to do a locator spell," said Amanda.

"Will it tell you how she is, if she's alright?" asked Brody.

"No, but it'll tell me where she is."

"How can I help?"

"Be here," Amanda smiled. "Right now, it's all we can ask and it's enough."

Brody sat there with worry. How could she say that so calmly? How could either of them just sit here when Sarina was out there with God only knew who? Was she being taken care of? Were her needs being met? Were the twins alright? What if she went into labor? There was no telling what would happen if she had the babies before she was rescued. Brody stood up… he needed to move around.

"I can't just sit here," Brody said, pacing, his fists clenched tight.

"Son," Romeo said. "I know exactly how you feel. I know what it is to be so pent up inside that you just want to hit someone or something. Right now though, Sarina needs you to focus that energy on helping us find her. You can't do that if you go off half-cocked. She'll need all of you when we find her, so stay here and try to relax while Amanda finds her. Once we know where she is, we'll work on a plan to find her and take down whoever it is who's holding her."

Brandt ran into Fenris as the old leader was headed toward his chambers.

"How goes the sabotage?" asked Fenris.

"Excellent," Brandt said. "I had their daughter this afternoon and then I brought her here. You'll have your war now, or Romeo will submit. Either way, Sarina will be mine and Traverse and Duscene will easily die in the melee."

"You seem awfully confident, pup," Fenris said, his aged brown eyes weary of leading. "What happens if Romeo and Brody don't submit and aren't killed?"

"They'll easily bow down to you when you present Sarina Traverse with a knife to her throat."

"Why not get her to mate with you instead? If she bites you during sex, she'll be by your side instead of that traitor Duscene. That'd throw a wrench in their plans, especially if her two pups turn out to be yours."

"Right now, I'd rather not send her into labor to find out. She's in a delicate way and after the screw session I had with her this afternoon, I doubt she's in any shape to take me on again, especially this soon."

"Well, we'll keep her as added collateral regardless of whether she mates with you or not."

"Do you mind if I have the night sir? I have a particularly lovely female in a cabin I'd like to see to."

"Take the night," Fenris grinned. "You've earned it."

Brandt checked on Sarina, who was sleeping, and then packed his bag and headed out. He took the longer route, watching warily for the Traverse clan. He knew by now, they had to be culling their resources. By this time tomorrow, he expected the first round of revenge.

Finding the cabin barely lit, he wondered if the woman was still there.

"Knock, knock," he said, tapping on the door. He kicked it open, looking around the inside. The small fire in the fireplace was barely lit and the cabin was getting chilly. Checking the bedroom, he found the woman he'd left, sleeping soundly. "Hey, beautiful."

Unlike the night before, she seemed much better tonight. She'd rested well and looked even more stunning. "I was afraid you'd forgotten me."

"Never, darling. I brought more food and water. Do you feel like eating with me?" asked Brandt.

She sat up and smiled. "I'm Carly. I know we didn't really get a chance to introduce ourselves before."

"I'm Brandt. It's very nice to meet you Carly." Brandt took out cheese, bread and a large hunk of ham. He sliced off huge chunks, chuckling when Carly took them from his hand and ate as if she hadn't tasted food in days. "Glad I packed so much. How are you feeling?"

"Besides hungry?" she grinned. "I feel pretty damn good. It's been forever since anyone treated me decent. I'm afraid I was rather used to being handed around and then discarded."

"It's a shame," he said, meaning it. "No one should ever be made to feel that way… man, woman, or wolf."

"I couldn't agree more."

"I brought you some warmer clothes," Brandt said, pulling three pairs of jeans, four shirts, two sweatshirts and a jacket from the bag. "There are shoes and socks in there as well."

"Thank you," she smiled. Brandt watched her lift the gown she wore over her body and inhaled when he got a good look at her naked body. He grabbed her wrist before she ever reached for the clothes. Standing, he pulled her close and with one hard look into her eyes, took her mouth as passion erupted in his loins. "Brandt," she whispered before he took her lips again.

His hands touched her flesh to ignite in her what just a look started in him. He cupped her breasts, circling her nipples until they peaked for him. Then he ran his tongue over them, sucking them gently into his mouth… her moans only driving him to take more. Walking her backward, Brandt pressed Carly up against the wall of the bathroom, his hand dipping impatiently between her thighs. He found her hot, wet center and sank two greedy fingers into that liquid heat. Her hips bucked against him as he found her clit with his thumb. Running circles around her swollen nub he kept his fingers sliding in and out of her, taking her higher with each penetration. She moved with him, her body trapped by the rhythm he set as he turned them both on. Bracing his free hand against the wall, Brandt leaned close, taking her mouth again. Her tongue slid eagerly past his lips, tangling willingly with his.

Then her hands began to pull at his clothes, as if doing so would stem the fire he'd built up inside her. Brandt pulled his fingers back and helped her strip his clothes off. He wasn't prepared for the moment when she dropped to her knees and eagerly took his length between her lips. Her tongue wrapped warmly around his shaft, pulling him deeper into the hot, wet depths of her mouth. He felt his tip hit the back of her throat and groaned as his body began to rev up. Running his hands into her hair, Brandt gripped the back of her head and moved his hips back and forth, thrusting into her inviting mouth. Over and over again he pressed his length into her mouth, moaning as his body moved toward climax.

The need to fill her was overpowering and Brandt was weak, too weak, to fight it. Pulling out of her mouth, he helped Carly stand. He turned her around and found her swollen folds with his wet cock. The first thrust was hard and deep, pressing him fully into her hot snatch. Then it was all movement and moaning. Flesh pressed hard against flesh as Brandt gripped her hips and continued to penetrate her in a rhythm that catapulted them toward completion. Her moans mixed with his as Brandt continued to assault her body, his cock filling her over and over again. His vision blurred as her wet folds pummeled him with sensations he literally couldn't get enough of. When her pussy clenched around him, Brandt spent himself into her, burying himself deep into her hot depths.

Chapter Five

Sarina woke to the cold and reached for Brody, only to realize he wasn't there and she wasn't home. The events of the last twenty-four hours came back to her as her heart sank into despair. She laid a protective hand over her swollen belly, wondering if she'd even be able to deliver her twins in the comfort of family. Stiffening her spine, she refused the tears that threatened to let loose a tidal wave. She was a Traverse and a Duscene, even if she and Brody weren't legally wed yet. He was her mate and for her, that was enough. It disgusted her to think that Brandt had been able to get past her defenses. The mere thought that the babies she carried could be his made her want to vomit all over again. Needing answers, Sarina dressed as best she could and stepped into unfamiliar territory. She found several corridors that led to who knew where. She moved quickly back to Brandt's quarters and tried to calm herself. What would her mother do if this was happening to her? With a small smile, Sarina knew her mother would simply cause a rock pile to close off all the hallways except the one that led outside.

Sarina took a deep breath and tried to calm herself. She sat on the bed and thought about Brody, about how much she loved him and their children. She made rhythmic circles on her belly trying to reach out to him.

"Do you hear me?" she called in her mind. "I'm here, please find me."

Sarina got a flash in her mind, a moment of sight. It was her parents and siblings all spread out, searching for her. Encouraged, she reached out to them as well, begging someone she loved to hear her, to find her. "Mama!" she screamed in her mind. Pain radiated through her head as another flash came to her. This one was of Brody, his face illuminated just long enough for Sarina to see the determined anger there. The next flash showed him sitting with a dark haired woman, his mouth sliding warmly over her tight nipple. Sucking in a breath, Sarina knew it wasn't real. If it was, it wasn't her Brody.

The flashes started to come faster as the pain began to subside. Her parents and Brody talking, planning. Her siblings waiting impatiently with her grandfather. All of them spread out, searching. Would they even think to look this deep into the woods? Would any of them think to use their wolves to help? She knew that only her father and perhaps Brody were capable of changing into their wolves without the full moon, but she was doubtless that it'd be enough to see her freed from this hell hole.

"I trust you're doing well," came a slimy voice that made Sarina cringe. Looking up she saw an old man who looked as if he had one foot in the grave and the other just waiting to push off the edge.

"Actually, doing well would imply that I'm happy and healthy. Since I'm about to burst with these twins and I'm definitely not happy, you should trust that I am doing anything but well."

"You've got a temper like your da," the old man said, his Irish accent coming out in his speech. "Rumor has it, he can be quite demonstrative when he wants to show his status or needs to remind someone of their place in the pack."

"A good leader doesn't have to resort to violence to remind his wolves where and what their place is," retorted Sarina.

"No," he agreed. "But every once in a while it gets the point across much clearer than the more menial ways. I've been around long enough to know a thing or two about being an alpha. From where I'm sitting, even your da has a few things to learn."

"And you think you're going to teach him those lessons, do you?" Sarina couldn't keep the sneer off her face, nor the laughter from her voice.

"You little witch," Fenris said. His hand cracked hard against her cheek, sending a shockwave of pain through her whole face.

"You'll live to regret that action," Sarina said, her whole body going light as a feather. She felt heat radiate through her body as if she'd been dunked in lava. It swam through her veins, causing her arms to lift up and outward, much like an old zombie walk from *Night of the Living Dead*. As her anger boiled inside, bolts of white hot fire shot from the tips of her fingers, relieving her body of the heat. Fenris, though old, managed to change in a matter of seconds and yelped as a bolt hit his tail, singing the hair.

Once he was gone, Sarina dropped back down onto Brandt's bed. Gone was any excess energy she'd felt in that moment of awakening. Now her body felt exhausted, the twins battering her insides as they continued their crazy, exponential growth. She still didn't know how her mother had endured her and her brother, Jason, pounding around like this.

"I can't find her," Amanda said, her voice wavering with concern. "Wherever they have her, it's either too far away, or sheltered. I can't see anything."

"Can you sense anything?" Romeo asked, his own resolve stretching thin. "Any sort of darkness in the air?"

"The woods are always a dark place beyond our borders. I never know if it's just because the area isn't ours to rule, or if it's because something more sinister roams out there."

Turning, Amanda found herself surrounded by Penelope, Elijah, Briana, and Lucia. "You should be resting," she said to Penelope.

"My niece, who happens to be pregnant, is missing. I'm rested enough for now."

"I couldn't begin to talk her into staying home," Elijah said.

"And you all came," she said, tears flowing freely now as they all took a turn hugging her.

"She's our family," Briana said simply. "Not to mention, I was the one to tell her she was carrying twins. How could I not come when someone's taken her?"

"Just so everyone's on the same page," Romeo called out loudly, "We believe that Sarina was kidnapped by someone she thought she knew, someone impersonating Brody or someone else perhaps. We don't have proof of this, but somehow someone got close enough to take her. Amanda is almost certain that she's beyond the borders of our pack, which means we'll be dealing with whoever rules the wooded areas and beyond. We stay in groups of four or more at all times. Those of us who can, need the powers we have, so stick close by. If you see anything out of the ordinary, or sense anything off, tell one of the leaders immediately so we can alert everyone. It's not our goal to lose anyone during this search, so be mindful of where you are at all times. Brody will be leading the Eastern border, Amanda and I will take the Western edge and everyone else will fill out between us. We'll move forward slowly, because while we want to find Sarina as quickly as possible, we don't want to miss any clues by moving forward too fast. Are there any questions?"

"Why does he get to lead?" a grumpy man asked. Romeo rolled his eyes in irritation.

"Because Sarina is his mate and unless you can make the change as quickly as he can, he leads."

Brody didn't need to be told to make the change in order for him to understand. Within a minute, he sported the dark coat of his wolf, his eyes sharp, focused. He sat down next to Romeo, a show of submission. He panted quietly while Romeo lifted a hand to pet his head. "Brody Duscene brought his pack to join ours and has shown a submissive attitude since then. He's worked hard to integrate his pack comfortably into ours and I won't stifle that by putting one of mine in the place that should be his. If it wasn't Sarina we were looking for, I might make a different call. As it is, Brody has the right to lead, wolf or man. If there's no other necessary questions, we need to split up and get started."

Brody took the Eastern section and stalked up and down the pathways that led deeper into the dark, wooded area outside the borders of the Delta pack. His ears picked up every nuance from the crickets that were just starting their songs to owls and other night creatures. His nose was to the ground even as the man inside scrambled to think of where someone would have taken her, who she'd let get close enough. His mind rewound to the conversation they'd had the night of the full moon.

"Hey baby," Brody said when she entered their room. "I missed you today."

"Seeing me this afternoon wasn't enough, huh?"

"What?" Brody asked. Sarina watched him pick through the closet, trying to find something to wear that wouldn't mind getting shredded tonight. "I didn't see you this afternoon."

"You don't remember stopping me out by the Schultz's and kissing me brainless?"

"Hon, I'd damn well remember if my lips had touched yours this afternoon," Brody smiled. Turning, he came toward her in a way that always made Sarina's heart jump. She'd never met a man who could master the prowler stance as fluidly in his male form as he did in his wolf form, until Brody that is. The man exuded confidence as if he was born with a natural well of it inside himself. It was a major turn-on for her.

"I'm telling you, babe. You were wearing jeans and a t-shirt and your hair was all messy. Then you pulled me close and kissed me as if I was your last breath. Hot as hell if you ask me."

"Sorry I missed it," Brody grinned. "But I'm telling you, doll, that I was with your dad up until about an hour and a half ago… well past the time you're saying you saw me. Not that I'm not obliged now to make it up to you. I don't want you getting disappointed and letting strange men take liberties with you."

It came to him then, like a flash of hair scorching lightning. Sarina wasn't the type to let anyone close, unless she knew them. What if she had seen him that afternoon just as she'd said? Sitting on his haunches, Brody gave an ear piercing howl that echoed through the woods. Penelope was there within seconds. "You found something?"

"I think I may have figured out who took her," Brody said, pulling on jeans as he spoke. "Sarina wasn't one to let anyone close she didn't know. The fact that I was even on her radar was astounding once I started thinking about it. Whoever has her, looks and smells and acts like me. He's not me, but he did at least a convincing enough job to have Sarina going with him somewhere. If that's the case, she wouldn't have been able to know and that's why she told me she saw me the other afternoon. She did, except it wasn't me she saw. Romeo's right. Our pack has been infiltrated by whomever took Sarina."

"I'll let them know. Call again if you find anything else."

"Will do," Brody agreed. Standing behind a tree, he stripped down and became his wolf again, leaving his clothes for another pack member to grab. Brody continued his search, knowing that every mile they checked brought him closer to finding Sarina and his twins. He heard a long, loud howl that ripped through the air and made the hair on his neck and back stand straight up.

Penelope showed up again, her pretty eyes serious. "Romeo found a trail of Sarina's hair," she said.

"Where?"

"About a mile west of your current location," she said.

"Tell him we're on our way."

"I'll let him know," she said, hope illuminating her eyes. Brody watched her closely. Just as she'd come both times, she was gone with a huge gust of wind. Of all the Radiants, Penelope and Amanda were Sarina's family and although he knew she loved Briana and Lucia like aunts as well, he found Penelope and Amanda's powers to be the most helpful, especially right now.

Brody fought the urge to run ahead. A leader never left his people behind and he wasn't about to start now. He had his clothes put down and quickly made the change to a human again. As he pulled on a t-shirt, stretching the fabric over lean abdominal muscles, someone brought him food he could scarf down on the run. Already having changed four times, his metabolism had easily burned through thousands of calories that would leave him weak and unprepared if he didn't tank up on the way.

Twenty minutes later, Brody arrived with his entire squad of pack members. The man who'd questioned his leadership stepped up to him before he could address Romeo. "I just wanted to say that I judged you wrong. I'm glad to have you in our pack and on our side."

Brody shook the man's hand before turning to Sarina's father. "You found her?"

"Not yet," he said, but added a grin. "But my girl's got brains. Risky or not, she left a trail of her hair for us to follow. My nose found it, but I'm not sure it's as sensitive as it used to be. Do you want to try and track it?"

Brody changed instantly, forgetting to save his clothes. His wolf would have to do and anyone who saw him change back would have to excuse him. Sticking his nose in Romeo's hand, he picked up Sarina's scent and howled as he set off down the path, sniffing the ground here and there as he went. Every so often he'd howl, letting everyone else know where he was and which way the trail led.

Brandt returned to his pack's base as the sun was just coming up. He'd spent the early morning hours with Carly, making love in a way he'd never imagined could turn him on. He'd always been one for rough, mind-blowing sex. Then Carly had straddled him that morning and taken him slowly. Her need superseded his urge to drive her fast to climax and Brandt found a way of doing the deed that left a drop of sweetness afterward.

Still, he knew he had to deal harshly with his ward, or face the consequences Fenris would surely dole out to him if he didn't. "Get up!" he shouted, obviously startling Romeo's daughter from her sleep.

"I'm awake," she replied.

"I said to get up," he growled. "I've heard that you tried to set Fenris on fire. That, my darling, was a very big mistake on your part."

"Screw you," Sarina spat. Brandt hit her so hard across her cheek that she yelped in pain and fell against his bed.

"Don't you dare backtalk me, girl. You'll remember your place."

"My place is by my mate's side, welcoming our children into the world, enjoying time with my family. The longer you rob me of that, the worse your punishment will be. I can guarantee you that."

"And you think just because you're carrying those rats that it'll spare you from my punishment?"

Brandt grabbed her by the hair and dragged her out of the room. Down one long corridor, he shoved her into a room where the only decoration was a long mirrored wall. Soon the lights went out and Sarina was blinded by a spotlight. "Sarina, this is Dankar. Dankar, this is Sarina, the Delta pack's alpha's eldest daughter. Dankar is the man responsible for making me into your mate, or at least the vision and musky scent of him. Dankar is a wizard with black magic and he's gladly agreed to demonstrate some for you. Hold onto your panties, because your worst nightmares are about to become reality."

Brandt, confident that Sarina would be well taken care of and knocked down a few pegs, left her in Dankar's care with explicit instructions to keep him posted should anything develop from the treatment he'd use on her. He wasn't above hurting her to keep her in her place, but he'd prefer to keep the babies right where they were at the moment. Once she was back with her

family, she could deliver twenty babies if she wanted
for all he cared. He'd gladly give up his parental rights
if either twin turned out to be his, which he sincerely
hoped they weren't, even if it would help Fenris get the
war he wanted.

Chapter Six

Sarina stood in the dark room, waiting for whatever Dankar was going to throw at her. After her alternate reality visions, she figured there wasn't much that could scare her. She knew her twins were safely snuggled inside her womb and she also knew her family was searching for her. They'd find her eventually, everything else she could survive. "Do your worst, you son-of-a-bitch!"

"You'll wish very soon that I hadn't," the small man said. Sarina had no idea how he'd come within inches of her, but she knew when the needle pricked her arm that things were going to go from bad to much, much worse. She felt her body going weak as the black abyss of unconsciousness sucked her down into its hard depths.

"Sarina?" She heard her name as it was called again and again. "Sarina?"

Sarina opened her eyes to the noise, seeing her bedroom as she remembered it. She reached down and felt a flat abdomen, her heart kick-starting in her chest for a minute. "Mama!" she called back, tossing back the covers.

"There you are," her mother chuckled. "These two want their mother."

"Oh!" Sarina gushed, grabbing both of her babies and nuzzling them. She planted kisses all over their faces until they started to protest. "I've missed you babies. I feel as if I've been sleeping forever."

"You and Brody had a night out and from the looks of things, you didn't get to bed too early," Amanda said grinning. "After ten years together, however, I suppose any couple might want a special night out once in a while."

"Ten years?" Sarina asked, her mind reeling as two young boys ran into her room.

"Mom!" they both called.

"Slow down," Amanda demanded, halting both the boys in their tracks. "How do you expect your mother to hear you if you can't even stand still to talk to her?"

"Yes, Nana," the boys said in unison.

"What is it?" Sarina asked, trying desperately to grasp that these two beautiful handsome boys were the first set of twins she and Brody had made together. Different as night and day, it was stunning to know they were twins.

"Bradley called me a pussy."

"Did not!" the smaller of the two said, his face so much like his father's that Sarina grinned. "All I said was that Derrick acts like a pussy sometimes. He's always so damn sensitive about everything."

"First of all, young man, we don't talk like that. You will apologize to your brother and from now on, you'll keep your opinions to yourself. And since you think you need to share them so freely and with disrespect for your brother; you can also clean both bathrooms."

"Aw, Mom!" Bradley complained and he gave his brother a half-hearted apology. Sarina watched him trudge off to do his chores as if someone had stolen every ounce of his happiness.

That night, after she'd put her children to bed and tucked all of six of them in, she climbed into her bed next to Brody.

"Have I told you how beautiful you are lately?" he asked.

"Not today," she smiled.

He leaned over and kissed her, whispering it against her lips. "You still take my breath away."

Their second kiss turned things up a notch as Sarina melted into him. Just as his hand cupped her breast, Sarina was yanked violently back to the dark room, her body reeling. She squatted low and lost the little food she'd eaten, vomiting in a can on the floor.

Standing back up again she went to cuss out Dankar when pain radiated through her abdomen. Within minutes her water broke and Sarina felt the babies in her womb move into position. "Help me!!" she pleaded.

Brody led the way as the trail veered hard to the left as the trees gave way to acres and acres of grassland. Slowing down, Brody followed Sarina's scent into the mountains, fighting to keep it in front of him. It ended up against a flat face of the mountain that spiked high into the clouds and Brody scraped at the edge of the rock face, whining as he did so.

"It's alright," he heard Romeo say as his father-in-law laid a hand on his back. Brody sat on his haunches, both in submission and as a way to keep his impatience from showing. "We've found her now and we're not leaving without her. However, we need to be smart about this. If we mount a counter-strike, it's got to cripple their leader. After that, I can take over this band and add them to the Delta, if they're so willing. If not, we kill them. Anyone who stands against us is an enemy and not to be trusted."

Brody sensed movement on the other side of the rock face and gave a low growl, standing back up and pawing the ground again.

"Let's move back off to the woods and see what comes out of this thing come dawn," said Romeo.

Brody hated the waiting. Without any clothes to speak of, he was forced to stay in his wolf even as hunger clawed at him. He'd eaten all the food anyone could spare and still wanted to rip someone apart just to devour them. He sat at Romeo's side, whining with impatience. "Easy boy," Romeo said. "It won't be long now and I can guarantee you if I see someone who looks like you step out of that cave, you have first dibs."

Dawn finally came with a strong sun peaking over the mountains as the Delta pack waited. Brody was thankful to have nearly all of Sarina's entire family with him. Her parents, siblings, aunts and uncles and most of her cousins stood with him as he waited anxiously to get his mate back. He prayed he was fast and stealthy enough to keep her and his twins safe and healthy.

"She's hurting," Amanda said, stepping up to Romeo and Brody. "Wherever she is in there, she's in pain. I can't tell what from."

Brody gave a low, feral growl just as the rock face opened up. Werewolves, in the form of men, clamored from the cave, seeking the light and the freedom to stretch their legs. Brody and Romeo, in wolf form, took out the two who moved furthest from the cave and worked their way inward until they caught the two standing guard. Before they could give warning, Brody leapt on one, baring his teeth and pressing his massive black paw against the man's throat. Romeo had tackled the other one, standing over the stunned guard, baring his teeth just inches from the man's face. They waited for Amanda to join them.

"My husband and alpha of the Delta pack, would very kindly like to know where our daughter is. You have thirty seconds to tell us before he rips out your throat." When the man took too long, Romeo raked a claw across the man's windpipe, ending his life.

"Well?" she said to the man who was under Brody's heaving body.

"Brandt brought a woman in the other night. She looks like you only she's with child. I heard someone say this morning that she'd gone into labor. If that's true they would have taken her to Dankar's quarters at the back of the caves."

"Thank you," Amanda said, touching Brody's coat. Brody let the man up and growled at him. Then he chased the poor kid halfway through the woods before he returned to work with Romeo.

"We need to do this as stealthily as possible," he said.

"I can't do a locator spell necessarily, but I can get a look at the caves from here. Maybe I can work out a map of sorts for you two to follow."

"Let's do it," Romeo said, giving a regal shake of his head to denote his leadership for anyone who might think to question him.

Romeo ordered everyone to give Amanda space, except for the other Radiants who joined her without needing to be prompted. "Your powers will work better with all of us here," Penelope said, her voice brooking no argument.

"Powers of the earth," Amanda started.

"Powers of the wind," Penelope added.

Briana and Lucia added fire and water to the mix as their powers stretched out to the four corners of the earth. He stood in awe, as always, when Amanda took hold of her powers. Her body began to glow white as she etched out in the dirt a detailed map of the caving system where Sarina was being held. Quick, jerky movements of her eyes laid down tunnels and chambers that coursed through the elaborate system this pack used to house their members. When she stopped and their powers came back to them, it was like sucking the air out of a room before everything returned to normal.

"She's back here somewhere," Amanda pointed, showing the alternate routes the men could take to get to her. "I don't know whether it's best to go in as wolves, or try your luck as men. I'd say though that you're likely to be known as Romeo the man. Not too many here would recognize you in your wolf."

"She makes the best argument for it," Romeo said, looking at Brody.

"I won't control my wolf if someone's hurt her," Brody warned, nearly growling as he talked.

"No one's asking you to, son," Romeo assured him. "You can bet your ass, I'll be taking my time with the ones responsible for my daughter's suffering. Not to mention that of my grandchildren."

"Shall we?" Brody asked, stepping up to the opening of the rock face. "How do we get in?"

"Let me see if I can help," Amanda said. She touched the rock face and commanded the mountain to give up its secrets. The mirage fell away and showed a dark hole. Brody shifted with Romeo and followed his alpha inside.

The dark gave way to a huge open area where men and women sat around talking. Several couples occupied some of the alcoves tending to more carnal needs as Romeo walked past them. Brody followed, keeping his urge to attack under control. It was likely that none of these pups had anything to do with Sarina's kidnapping.

Straining, Brody listened for Sarina's moans. If she was truly in labor, she'd be panting by now, especially if her delivery went anything like her mother's had twenty-five years earlier. They made it past the large gathering place and headed down the furthest tunnel, running past chamber after chamber. Brody heard a couple in their room engaging in what could only be described as passionate intercourse. Even in his first encounters with Sarina he wasn't sure he'd ever been that rough with her. Shaking his head to clear it, he headed on, catching Romeo's tail as they turned and headed down another corridor.

This one was danker, the musty smell irritating his nose. He sneezed but continued on. The floor under their paws turned cold and damp as they headed further and further into the mountain and it occurred to Brody that getting to Sarina would be a cinch compared to getting her back out again. He'd voice his opinion after they made it to her and secured both her and their babies. As they turned once again to the left, Brody heard the ear piercing sound of a woman in severe pain. Her scream turned to a grunt as Brody stopped outside a chamber that wasn't guarded in the least. His ears listened for the number of voices inside.

"You've got to push now, Sarina," came a soft, female voice. "These babies want to be born now. You can do this. You're an alpha's daughter."

Brody wanted to lick the woman for being tender to his mate, even as he wanted to rip her throat out for being here at all.

"She'll deliver them or I'll cut them out of her. Either way, she'll give birth today," came a nasty, edgy voice. Brody bit down on his growl even as his muscles bunched to attack. "She's got fifteen minutes to get that first brat out, or I'll do it for her."

Brody heard Romeo's growl of warning, but could no longer sit and hear this man berate his mate. He burst through the door, overwhelmed by the flood of lights that blinded his eyes. In an instant his eyes adjusted enough to see a very small man pointing a gun at him. "Down doggy," the man said, his voice grating on Brody's last nerve.

His low, feral growl was met with a silver bullet to his shoulder that all but crippled his leg. Yelping, he backed up two steps. Joined by Romeo though, Brody found the strength he needed. Growling loudly now, he charged the small man, who wouldn't have been half his height if Brody had been in his human form. Another silver bullet to his chest did nothing to slow him down and with one swipe, Brody ended what had passed for the smaller man's life.

His teeth sank deep into the man's throat, but unlike the rich flavor of human blood, all Brody tasted was the rancid flavor of death and darkness. The blood that poured over his muzzle was as black as coal and Brody tried desperately to get the taste out of his mouth. The smell assaulted his nose as he turned to see Romeo cornering the woman who'd talked to Sarina.

Immediately his eyes locked with hers and the man inside the wolf wept for her relative safety. Then he was changing back, to be the man Sarina needed. "You can do this baby."

"He's coming so fast," Sarina said. Another contraction caused her to bear down, her growl of exertion making Brody grin. Here was the woman he'd fallen in love with. Here was his mate. "Come on, Sarina," Brody said, moving down by her feet to catch his first born.

"Can you ask Amanda and Penelope to come?" inquired Brody as he looked at Romeo.

"On it," Romeo said, stepping discreetly from the room. Within a matter of minutes both Amanda and Penelope were there, moving everything where it needed to go.

"Brody, you just stay right there son," Amanda said in the most maternal tone he'd ever heard. "Pen and I will make sure everything's ready when that little guy comes along. Push now, Sarina."

One more contraction and Sarina delivered a beautiful, dark haired baby boy she readily named Brody Andrew Duscene. His brother, as light as Brody Jr. was dark, came along swiftly behind him. His given name was Jedidiah Bryan Duscene. Brody marveled at them, the complete and utter reliance they had on him and Sarina. At Amanda's instruction, Brody held baby Brody against his chest while Sarina took Jedidiah. Within an hour of delivering, Sarina was able to sit up and nurse both babies, surrounded by her family. Fenris and the remainder of his pack were nowhere to be found and while the moments following the twins' arrival were surreal, everyone felt the underlying current of tension that never quite went away. There would certainly be a war now and both Brody and Sarina knew they'd do whatever it took to protect their babies.

Chapter Seven

It took the night and well into the next day for Sarina to feel as if she could attempt the move home with the twins. She'd eaten and was well rested, considering she'd just given birth. Brody stayed by her side from the start, hovering like a love-struck pup. Not that she minded. The hours she'd spent away from him were enough to make his presence precious, not to mention, he carried little Brody in his arms. "I can't get over them," Brody said, grabbing Sarina's free hand. "Thank you."

"For what?"

"For being the most amazing woman I've ever known. I've never been so in love with you." Stopping her in her tracks, he let everyone else walk around them. He was still shirtless from his change, but Romeo had graciously found him a pair of jeans. Brody cupped her cheek, running his thumb down her jaw and over her lips. He took her mouth then, slowly seduced her to kiss him back.

"Brody," Sarina said, her bright green eyes shining. "Let's get these two home. Seeing you with him makes me want to cuddle you."

"I want to do more than cuddle you," he said, playfully slapping her ass.

<<<>>>

Sarina was ready to drop by the time they actually stepped through the door of their home. Brody gladly took Jedidiah from her and laid the twins together in their bassinet. Then he turned and scooped Sarina up into his arms, carrying her upstairs to their master bathroom. He drew a warm bath and gently lifted her into it. Keeping an ear out for the twins, Brody helped Sarina wash her body. He shampooed her hair and ran conditioner through it, enjoying the way she relaxed in the water.

"I never knew how amazing it'd be to hold them."

"I've never held anything that delicate. I've never fallen in love so quickly. One look and I was head over heels for them."

"They are incredible," Sarina agreed. She rested her head back on the tub and closed her eyes as Brody continued to take time with her hair. He rinsed the conditioner out, combed her long locks and then braided it down her back. Once that was done, he twisted it up into a bun that would get it out of her way and still allow her to look breathtaking while she cared for the twins. "I need to get something to eat," she said after half an hour of soaking.

Brody helped her stand and dress in the gown Amanda had given her. Apparently Amanda had worn that same gown when she'd first had Sarina and Jason.

The sentiment wasn't lost on his mate. "I want to get married."

She looked up at him as if he'd grown two heads. "Really?"

"Yes," he smiled. "I want all of my family to be Duscene's, no offense to your family."

"None taken. You and the boys are my family now. I just assumed that getting married wasn't a big deal for you."

"It wasn't," Brody admitted. "Until I watched the love of my life deliver my sons. I realized then that it matters a great deal to me that when people address you, they say Mrs. Duscene, instead of just Sarina or Miss Traverse. I want everyone to know that you're mine, that I'm the one who has the privilege of loving you."

"Brody," Sarina sighed. She wrapped her arms around his neck before she went on. "I need to tell you something that may not be easy to hear."

"Shoot, girl." Brody took her hand and walked with her downstairs to the kitchen. He poured her a cup of hot tea as she rummaged for food.

"The man who infiltrated us, the one who impersonated you… I thought he was you."

"I know," Brody said, taking her hand in his. He rubbed his thumb over her knuckles as she fought the wave of tears he saw coming. "Hey, it's alright. I know you didn't know. How can I blame you for something you didn't choose?"

"But I did choose," she cried. "I chose to go with him, to allow him to touch me, to take me. How could I not have seen that he wasn't you?"

"Sarina," Brody said patiently. "The man used a black arts magician to fake being me, changing and contorting his body to do so. He smelled like me, sounded like me, and for all intents and purposes, was me. I can't blame you for something you didn't do intentionally."

"I can't shake the feeling that somewhere deep inside I knew. He was rough in a way you never were, even in our most impatient times. I brushed it off as an overload of passion, but now I'm not so sure I didn't know."

Brody sighed. His mate was stressed out about things she couldn't change. "Sarina, I love you. I will always love you, no matter where we go, or what happens to us. Those two beautiful baby boys are ours and right now, being here with you and them is the only thing I care about."

<<<>>>

Life fell into a lovely routine of feedings, diaper changes, laughter, and general bliss for Sarina, Brody, and their twins. Brody, who at first would gag at the thought of changing his sons' stinky diapers, learned to move past the stench and do what needed to be done. He spent time talking to his boys while Sarina showered or took a nap, or even sat in the kitchen just enjoying a cup of tea.

Together, they loved and nurtured their sons through those first, crazy weeks of living. "Sarina!"

"Yeah?" she answered, still in her bathrobe with her hair falling in damp tendrils around her shoulders.

"Jedidiah needs a diaper change and Junior's got food all over him."

She sighed at the look on his face. He still looked so lost when it came to caring for both boys at once. "Give me Jedidiah. I'll bathe him and when you get Junior under control, you can trade off with me and get Jed dressed."

"Okay," he said, seeming relieved. By the time Sarina had bathed both boys and gotten Junior dressed, she had to spritz her hair with water to be able to do anything with it. She came back in the room just as Brody was laying their sleeping boys down on the bed. They worked to create a safe space for them and then slipped from the room quietly. "We're doing okay right?"

"Considering neither of us has ever been a parent before, I'd say we're doing excellent. Our children are well-fed, clean, healthy, and loved. Is there something else they need?"

She giggled when he wrapped an arm around her waist and pulled her closer, tugging at the tie on her robe. "I think they're good," he grinned. "We, on the other hand, are in desperate need of some adult entertainment."

"Adult entertainment, huh?" she smiled.

"Do you have any idea how many times, in just the past week, I've wanted you?"

"I've barely seen myself out of pajamas in the last week, how can you possibly want me?"

"I used to think, in the beginning that I couldn't possibly find you any more attractive. That there was no way that I could want you more. Then I watched you carry and deliver our babies and everything in me changed. I have such admiration and respect for you. Not that I didn't before, but now it's off the charts. And yes, Sarina, if it's at all possible, I find you ten times more attractive, even in pajamas, now, than I did before Brody Jr. and Jedidiah arrived."

He could have easily said something less honest, or blown off her statement. Instead he'd said exactly what she'd needed to hear. He'd told her that being a mother, bearing his children, was the sexiest thing she could do. Feeling endeared to him, Sarina pressed a smile to his lips and all but melted into his embrace. "Sarina," he whispered even as his mouth met hers again.

Fire flared inside her as if someone had placed a lit stick of dynamite inside her. Weeks of taking care of the boys had strained their intimate time to the breaking point and Sarina knew now that she wasn't the only one who'd felt it. Giggling, she wrapped her legs around his waist when he lifted her. He carried her easily into their spare bedroom, laying her down gently on the queen bed they'd just purchased. "We've been needing to break this bed in for a while now."

"Tell me about it," she said, her green eyes bright with desire. She watched with unabashed hunger as Brody stripped out of his shirt. She loved the look of him, the way his torso narrowed just at the hip and flared out at the shoulder so that she could rest her head there when she needed to. She reached a hand out to touch the tattoo he'd put on his ribcage of the boy's footprints. The inscription said: *Always remember them like this*. It was a reminder to them both that as parents it was their job to raise well-adjusted, respectful young men and to never forget how little they'd been once upon a time. To cherish every moment, no matter what age or stage their boys were in.

"This tattoo makes you look so damn sexy," she smiled, pressing her lips to his flesh.

"I like your boobs," Brody said, a boyish grin splitting his lips.

"You would," she laughed.

"I'm serious," he said, his blue eyes grinning with his smile. "They were wonderful before, but now that you're nursing the boys, they call to me. I'll catch you getting dressed in the morning or after a shower and all but bite my fingers off to keep from touching you."

"You can touch me now," she said, pulling him down to her. Brody wanted to do more than touch her. He wanted to consume her, to make her spontaneously combust. His hands actually shook when he placed them on her skin. Her body had gone through some serious changes in the last two months and Brody found those changes intoxicating. Her belly was soft where she'd carried the twins and stretch marks marked her body on her abdomen and breasts. He kissed her there, loving the feel of her warmth. It seemed she was always warm now, whether or not she was holding a baby. "I love you," he whispered, pressing a kiss just under her breast. Before she could respond, he closed his lips gently over her tight nipple, running his tongue over her flesh. He didn't suckle or spend too much time on her nipples, to keep her milk from running. He did make up for it in other ways though.

It'd been nine weeks since he'd taken her and the wait was next to killing him. Parting her robe completely, Brody just stared. Here was the woman who'd changed his life just by shopping with her family. That one single day, his whole life had done a 180 degree turn. Lying down beside her, Brody leaned close and took her mouth slowly, sliding his tongue over her lips. She met him hungrily, obviously as hungry as he was. Her hands found his chest and roamed over his skin, eventually finding the snap to his jeans. She undid them easily and slid her hand past his boxers, driving him half mad when her long, warm fingers circled him.

Before he knew it, she was straddling him, her breasts hanging over him as she worked his pants off. He touched them then, noticing the warm milk that dripped over his fingers. When she didn't come back up right away, he realized she'd stopped to put her bra back on. Already he knew he'd miss her breasts. He could sacrifice a year without them for his sons, couldn't he? Grinning he pulled her back up to him, anxious to feel her now that they were both naked.

The instant his tip touched her wet folds, Brody filled her. Gently he took her, letting her lead him as she rose up and slid back down. His cock throbbed at the hot wetness and her body, the way she clenched around him drew moans from him he couldn't keep in if he tried. She was a goddess and Brody figured he was lucky to have her. She cupped her own breasts, her breathless moans, stirring his own need. Pulling her close and tight, Brody reversed their direction so she was beneath him. Rocking just his hips back and forth, Brody filled her over and over again. They went slowly, each learning to love the other in a completely new way, post parenthood. Still, her warmth drove him mad as his mouth found hers. He pressed his thumb against her clit and had her hips bucking hard against his, taking him fully into her depths. Again and again Brody stroked her, giving her a rhythm that sent her spiraling out of control as her orgasm rocketed through her. Unwilling to wait, Brody gripped her hips and almost violently pumped himself into her, his own orgasm making him see stars as he tried to hold on to her.

She rolled to her side when he moved and Brody found a comfortable spot behind her, pulling her close. They stayed like that for a while before she turned to look at him. "Do you think it'll always be like this with us?"

"What do you mean?"

"Do you think we'll always be this ravenous for sex?"

"Probably not," Brody said practically. "The boys will get older and our sex life will probably go back to a steadier schedule. I'm not saying we won't have this level of need or passion. I just think it'll be easy to be intimate once the boys are a little older."

"Oh," she said, her face falling.

"Sarina," Brody grinned. "Whether I have you two times a day or two times a month, I will always want you. I will always seek to pleasure you. That won't ever change, no matter how often we're together."

"I just don't feel sexy," she said, finally voicing the concern he'd seen earlier.

"You should," Brody encouraged. "You should feel on top of the world. You're a hero. You've done something that somehow should be impossible and isn't. You brought two, beautiful, healthy boys into the world. You turned our love into two tiny beings. Not to mention that you feed them from your own body. I'd give you the damn Nobel Peace Prize for achievements in scientific impossibilities if it was up to me."

She laughed, a sound Brody had been waiting to hear. It wasn't the sort of laugh that's done in grace after a bad joke, but rather the full-on belly busting laugh that made him laugh along with her. "The Nobel Peace Prize," she chortled. "God I love you. You always know what to say to make me laugh. How do you do that?"

"I'm your better half, as you are mine," he grinned, capturing her mouth in a playful kiss. "Why don't we go check on the boys and try to enjoy some quiet time downstairs?"

"Does quiet time include ice cream?"

"A smidge," Brody agreed. "With bananas and chocolate syrup."

"Yum," Sarina smiled.

Chapter Eight

Fenris was furious with his pack. The mere fact that those deviants had taken out four of his finest guards and exiled two more, was so grating that he'd confined everyone in his pack to solitary confinement in their cells with the assurance that he'd execute anyone who disobeyed. How the hell was he going to replace Dankar? The man had worked for him for years and they'd felled him with one swipe. And they'd managed to help that bitch deliver her pups and make an escape, all while he'd been making plans to undo the great Romeo and his bloody pack.

He stalked up and down his chambers, loathing his weak pack. If he had even one person with the potential to be an alpha, just maybe he'd be able to make things right again. Just maybe his plans wouldn't go to hell in a hand basket. Rewinding the events of the breach of his caves by Romeo's Delta pack, Fenris caught a piece of information that, until now had eluded him. Where the hell was Brandt? The little bastard had been turned into the spitting image of Brody Duscene and he was nowhere to be found.

It'd be the last time he gave that little prick a twenty-four hour reprieve. Twenty-four hours and two months was a little extreme to his way of thinking. Taking some deep breaths, Fenris thought about the different angles he could use to get to Romeo's pack. Plenty of them were in the outskirts of the main town. He could try to win them over, but wasn't sure they'd be all for giving up their nice homes to live in a cave. His one attempt to take a Traverse heir had failed miserably. He hadn't even been able to keep one of the pups she'd borne.

Romeo Traverse was a literal pain in his ass, Fenris thought as he continued to brood. Perhaps there was another way around this whole war business. With the full moon coming around again, Fenris knew that all the male wolves would change, no matter whose pack they belonged to. If his wolves waited outside town and intermixed with the Delta pack, they could easily dispatch quite a few of Romeo's recruits by morning.

It wasn't the war he'd wanted, but a solid battle to be sure. Still, it required more thinking and much, much more planning.

Brandt sat with Carly as they ate breakfast. They'd mated during his twenty-four hour reprieve from the caves and Brandt, upon returning, had seen the caves destroyed. So, he returned to the small cabin in the woods to be with Carly full time. It'd taken some getting used to for her, once the spell Dankar had put on him wore off. He'd been sure she'd hate him, but if anything, she seemed even more attracted to him.

As for her, he'd learned that she was twenty-six, a year younger than him. She'd been abandoned as a pup because she was half the size of her sister and so had been passed around from male to male in the pack that adopted her, once she reached her first breeding season. She'd miscarried several times and was exiled from the pack because she couldn't carry a baby full term.

It had nearly broken Brandt's heart to know that the men of her pack had used her so carelessly. Still, he couldn't say he was without blame. He'd done virtually the same thing to Sarina Traverse. To this day he still didn't know if either of her children had been fathered by him. He'd come clean to Carly about his role, especially after the spell had vanished. She'd understood that he'd been acting under Fenris' orders and even forgiven him when he explained that it had been his idea, to try and move up the ranks of the pack.

"Everyone does what they must to survive," Carly had said, her sparkling brown eyes full of understanding.

"I'm sorry you had to do so much," Brandt had replied. Since then, he and Carly had made the cabin a home, cleaning out anything they didn't like and adding the things they did. Brandt had gathered more lumber and was working on adding some serious square footage to the now, one room, one bath dwelling. He knew if he showed his face in the Delta, he'd probably be executed on the spot, although he was pretty sure no one knew what he really looked like. He also knew that if he tried to return to his pack, he'd be beaten within an inch of his life, so that option was out as well. The only option left was to try and make the best life he could for him and Carly in the woods that stood between the pack he'd infiltrated and the pack he'd left. It wasn't the choicest real estate, but it'd have to do as there were literally no other alternatives.

He often wondered how Sarina was doing with the twins. He figured by now, even if one of the twins looked exactly like him, she wouldn't give him up. Not that he really wanted to parent a baby, but at times he wondered if one of them had turned out to be his. Carly hadn't liked what he'd done in trying to get a woman he wasn't mated to, pregnant, but she knew well how people used what was at their disposal to get what they wanted.

"You feel like going for a walk?"

"Sure," Carly answered. Brandt took her hand and together they walked through the woods, picking up broken bits of branches and such for their stove back home. Brandt had come across some old abandoned cabins and one had a nice wood burning stove inside. He'd taken it for the cabin as paying for electricity for that location was out of the question. He'd brought Carly the second time he went and she'd found some items she used to decorate the cabin. He hoped to have the room and roof finished before winter set in. It would be nice to expand and feel as if they weren't sitting on top of each other all the time.

As they walked, Brandt kept an ear out for any sign of another pack's members. He couldn't just start his own pack, but neither did he want to run into a member of Fenris' pack or those from the Delta pack either. He was walking a fine line of existence and he knew it.

<<<>>>

"You look amazing," Amanda said to her eldest daughter as she rocked Brody Jr. to sleep. "And these two little ones are what a woman dreams of when it comes to having grandchildren. I couldn't ask for more than this."

"Brody said that it didn't matter who their biological father was. He understood how it all happened and said he doesn't care, as long as we're all together."

"You found yourself a great mate, Sarina," Amanda smiled. "I was worried in the beginning, I'll admit that. But Brody has shown his love for you time and time again. The man seems to know that love is a verb and he works it out for you often enough. I'm beyond happy for you."

Sarina put Jedidiah down with Brody Jr. on a makeshift bed Amanda had made up on the floor of the living room so she'd be close by. Then she went in search of her husband. She figured he was with the rest of the others.

"I thought I might find you out here," she said, reaching out to touch Brody's shoulder. When he turned toward her though she looked into dark, soulless eyes that scared her down to her core. She blinked and when she opened her eyes again, Brody was staring back at her.

"You alright, hon?" he asked.

"Yeah," she said. "Just a little light headed I guess. How are you two doing out here?"

"We're great," Jason said, a grin splitting his face.

"Your brother's just happy because he keeps whooping my ass at volleyball," said Brody.

"We are damn good," Sarina laughed. "Where'd dad go? Maybe we can do pairs and show these two how it's done."

"We've never played together, babe."

"Yeah, but it'll be fun learning. Besides, I could use a little down time and beating my brother always feels good."

"She's ruthless," Romeo said, catching the ball Jason tossed to him. "Watch out."

"I'm not ruthless," Sarina smiled. "I'm just that good."

"Conceited is more like it," Jason teased, earning him a playful punch from his twin.

"Bring it on then," she challenged. "If we win, y'all have to fix us dinner. If you two win, Brody and I will repaint the house."

"Repaint the house?" Brody objected. "You know I'm going to get stuck with that, you have the twins to take care of."

"That's exactly how she works man," Jason snickered. "She makes it seem as if she'll help and then, Bam! You're stuck doing her part too."

"Oh please," Sarina complained. "How many times did I clean up after you so you could go chase tail?"

"I had to work at it obviously. I'm the same age as you and still haven't found my mate. You walk out of a store and find yours. I'd say we're square."

"They'll never stop bickering if we don't start playing," Romeo smiled. "All grown up and they still fight like week old pups."

Sarina and Brody did well, holding their own against an obviously better paired, Romeo and Jason. They lost graciously and agreed to help Romeo with some chores around the house. Repainting was off the list as Sarina couldn't help with the job, but nonetheless they all had a great time.

Two weeks later, Sarina was just getting out of the shower when she heard Brody Jr. and Jedidiah crying. "Brody!" she called, pulling on her bathrobe and going to the bedroom to pick up the babies. She calmed them down and went to see where Brody was.

"Brody?" she said, noticing him standing in the kitchen. "Didn't you hear the babies crying?" Moving around Brody, Sarina saw a blank stare on his face and his eyes were that same dark color again. It sent chills down her spine. "Brody?"

Sarina touched his shoulder again and saw his eyes flash back and forth between that dark, scary abyss and the blue she loved. "Hey baby," he smiled. "You finally get done with your shower?" Sarina watched him turn and act as if nothing had happened, pulling cereal from the cupboard and making himself breakfast.

"Brody, what happened to you?"

"What do you mean, doll?"

"When I got out of the shower, the babies were crying and when I came down here, you were just standing here, staring off into space. And for the second time now, I've seen your eyes turn to black pools of scary nothingness."

"Don't worry, babe," he assured her. "I'm great, but I haven't been sleeping well lately. Maybe I should sleep in the guest room after you head to bed with the twins."

"If you think it'll help you with whatever's going on with you, then I don't mind. I just don't want to see your health fall apart from something as silly as bad sleep. I don't care if we have to take different shifts with the babies, as long as you're really okay."

"I'm fine," Brody assured her, pressing a kiss to her forehead.

Brody ate breakfast and then kissed Sarina and the boys before he headed outside to work. He worked in the yard and surrounding area until his muscles ached and he'd soaked his shirt through with sweat. Winter would be here before they knew it and he wanted Sarina to be free from worry about the house or yard.

Looking toward the big picture window he saw her dancing with the boys to some rhythmic song he couldn't hear. He sighed knowing that he'd lied to her that morning. He wasn't fine and he was at a loss as to what to do about it. He was having blackouts, time lapses, and nightmares.

The nightmares always started the same. He would be overlooking the Delta, his vision taking in the expanse of every pack member from the river to town and up to the Traverse mansion. He could hear them all, laughing and loving in their homes. Then the hate would boil up in him. Try as he might, he couldn't fight the extreme revulsion that would swamp him. It didn't matter if he was thinking of just Romeo and his family or the entire Delta pack, or some other singular family; he hated them all with a level of feeling untouched by any other.

Then he'd hear his name. *Brody*. It'd slither through his brain and turn him on, even as she appeared before him. He didn't know who she was, or what she wanted, but he knew that she was the epitome of evil. Still, in the nightmare he couldn't fight her off. Whatever power she held was much too strong. Whatever she wanted, he gave her. Whatever she asked, he did. And there was a sick feeling in his stomach that his nightmares were becoming real.

Taking a sip of water, Brody coughed, feeling something stuck in his throat. He coughed again and again, finally dislodging whatever had been stuck and spitting it on the ground. Bending down to examine it, he saw a smear of blood on his hand, tasted the heavy metallic flavor of iron. He rinsed his mouth out and headed inside to talk with Sarina.

"You hungry? I was just about to make supper."

"I'm okay, I'll eat later. I was hoping you had a minute to talk," Brody said, preparing himself.

"Sure, babe. What's up?"

"I need to apologize to you, because I lied to you earlier. You asked me if I was okay and I said I was, when really I'm not. Something is happening to me and I have no idea how to stop it, but I'm damned sure if I don't find a way, it's going to destroy me and anyone who's close to me."

"What do you mean?" she asked.

Brody told her about the blackouts, the waking daydreams, and the hellish nightmares. He told her about the woman who always appeared to him and how she made him feel.

"It's like being a prisoner, except she can rule my body. She's a highly sexual being and whatever it is she wants, she somehow thinks I can get it for her, or give it to her. She scares the shit out of me, Sarina and still, there's a part of me that's extremely attracted to her in the nightmare. She makes me want her."

"We need to see my mother and father," Sarina said. Without another word, she went to grab Brody Jr. and Jedidiah, packing them in their car seats and helping Brody put them in their SUV. They made the short trip easily and then, with everyone else minding their own, sat down to talk with Romeo and Amanda.

"It sounds to me like a sort of possession," Amanda started, having heard Brody's side of things. "She…whoever she is, wants to use you to get something from our world, or to get here. Have you noticed anything different, anything that could have caused this transfer of energy?"

Brody instantly thought of the moment when he killed Fenris' black magician. The way his black blood had filled his mouth and overtaken his senses. *Brody*, came the sultry voice from his nightmares, infiltrating even his waking hours. *Tell them nothing, Brody.*

"Not that I know of," he lied, again. "I feel fine, except for when I black out or sleep."

"Have you had contact with anyone, besides the wolves at the caves, and our pack, since we got back?"

"No," he replied. "I just want to figure out what's happening to me. I don't want to risk Sarina or the twins, if this thing gets out of hand."

"We're not going to let it get that far," Amanda assured him. She mixed dry herbs in a bowl to make a poultice. "Make this tea and drink it before you go to bed tonight and when you wake up in the morning. I can't guarantee it'll expel her, but maybe it will quiet her enough that you can sleep. When your symptoms return, come see me for more. Maybe we can irritate her enough that she leaves you."

"Thank you," Brody said, unsure of how to feel about the whole thing.

Chapter Nine

Fenris gathered his pack together the night before the full moon, in the largest room he had. He hadn't returned to the caves yet, so space was limited. "As many of you know, our wonderful magician, Dankar, was ruthlessly murdered by the Delta pack this July. If for nothing else, we owe them retribution for his death. Tomorrow night is the full moon and I want as many of you as possible to make the change. Every male in our pack, of course, will do this, but the females as well. If you're not expecting, then you too will change. I want to infiltrate their borders and slay as many of them as possible. If we can't get to their men, we'll take their women and children. No one survives. A decent strike to their heart ought to get this war started and there's no better way to accomplish that, than to hurt their hearts."

The members of Fenris' pack spent the day planning their individual attack plans. Each one responsible, either as an individual or as a couple, to take down one or two of the outlying homes on the Delta pack's radar. "These are the outer most layers of Romeo's pack," Fenris said, circling about twenty homes on the outskirts of town. "If we can plunder all of them tomorrow night while their men are off enjoying the change, we'll deal a serious blow to both their numbers and their morale. Their men won't want to leave their wives and children after tomorrow night and the ones who lose their mates won't have the will to fight."

"What if the women make the change to guard their children?" one woman asked.

"Are we so weak that we can't get past a changing female?" Fenris chuckled derisively. "We will force their hand in this," he added. "Or we'll damn well die trying."

On the morning of the full moon, Fenris walked the entire line, making sure his wolves were in position far enough out that Romeo's pack wouldn't notice them. They each had food and water rations to sustain them through the day and were ordered to keep a sharp eye come nightfall. "If you have anything that needs to be done beforehand, get it done. I want you all sharp and ready when the moon rises."

The moon started its ascent over the horizon as Fenris waited. He'd given strict orders that his pack was not to howl at the full moon, no matter how strong the urge. It was a crime he made sure they knew was punishable by death, without so much as a question being asked. Walking his first strike line, he tapped the first couple to move and laughed heartily when the sounds of screaming reached his ears. His wolves returned, their muzzles coated in blood. "Good," he said. He moved on, tapping each consecutive individual or couple and the results were astounding. Romeo's pack was going to be devastated come dawn. He had a couple of courageous females turn to protect their children and the battles had been intensely gratifying. Despite the scratched and bruised bodies, Fenris' wolves had done well, dispatching the mothers and their children with relative ease. As dawn crept closer, Fenris and his pack retreated into the woods, close enough to hear reports of their deeds, but far enough away that they wouldn't be detected. After they got their reports, they'd make their way back to their new home and wait.

Sarina paced all over her parent's sitting room, her nerves stretched thin. She'd gone out early with Brody Jr. and Jedidiah, letting her mate sleep. On her normal walk she often visited the outlying pack members to ensure they were well taken care of. She'd come upon the Schultz home to see Alexander sitting on the steps, rocking back and forth, incoherent. When she got close he growled at her, low and feral, a look of terrible despair on his face.

"Alex?" she said, not reaching out to touch him.

"I shouldn't have left them," he mumbled. "They'd still be here if I hadn't left them."

"Did something happen to Christy and the girls?"

"They're dead," he said, as if quoting a news headline. "Slaughtered by wolves, by the looks of it. And not ordinary wolves either. This was a hit from another pack."

"What?" Sarina asked, marching past him and barely making it a step past the doorway. The stench of blood and death soaked the walls of the entrance. Pieces of hair and skin were strewn everywhere and Sarina closed her eyes, not wanting to see anymore. Before she could stop herself, she shoved the stroller away and retched in the grass. Wiping her mouth she gently touched Alexander's arm. "Will you come with me? Come and speak with my father. If this was another pack's doing, we need to prepare for whatever comes next."

"There is no next for me," he said. But he followed her anyway. He wasn't the only one to follow her that morning. Before she'd gone halfway along her usual route, Sarina knew that there would be tens, maybe hundreds more. She collected Tom Anders, Ben Jackson, Sheldon Pickett, and Grady Thompson, somehow seeing them through their grief, to her parent's home.

"Sarina?" Amanda said, a look of worry on her face when she took in her daughter and the men that followed her.

"Oh, Mama," she cried. "It's terrible!" Sarina recounted, as best she could, the scenes she came upon. All nearly uniform with the ruthless killing of werewolves.

"My God," Romeo breathed, not wanting his anger to show. After they'd seen the men upstairs to rest, with a little help from Amanda's sleep medication, Romeo finally spoke. "This is Fenris' doing. He's wanted a war for a long time, hitting us under the belt so to speak with his imposter. We snatched you back with the twins and now he wants the big show."

"You're not going to engage him, are you?" asked Sarina.

"No," Romeo said. "Not as he expects anyway. He wanted to hurt our family and he has aimed with deadly precision. However, we won't give him the war he wants. I will go to him and I will speak with him. I am sure he wants my submission and to take over the Delta. I will die before I see that happen. However, I will find out what it is he's after besides power. He's aging rapidly now and there's no telling how far his plans will go."

"He'll kill you if you go alone," said Amanda.

"I'm not going alone," Romeo said. "But I have to be wise in my choices. If I take all the men with me, who stays to protect the women and children? Fenris' pack has gone to great lengths to show us that they do not value the lives of females and their offspring. It is my intent to take him and his entire pack down without a war. I won't, however, see my family in jeopardy to make that happen. We need to think and to plan very, very carefully."

Romeo had Amanda and Penelope attend to the men who'd lost their families while he and his brothers, his sons, Jason, Wade and Joshua, worked on a strategy. "We can't fight them and win if all we're after is revenge," Elijah said.

"The hell we can't," Bryce said, always the one to argue the point. "They decimated some of our most prominent families, in the middle of the night, on a full moon. If that doesn't require one on one, I don't know what does."

"We need more to go on than just *run in, hack-hack, die*," Sebastian said, his dark eyes just as angry as everyone else's.

"What do you suggest?" Joshua asked. "We were expecting something from them and they still out-maneuvered us."

"Then perhaps we shouldn't attack, at least not yet," said Sebastian.

"You expect the men who lost their families to accept that?" Bryce growled.

"I don't expect anything from anyone. I'm just trying to offer alternative solutions," Sebastian countered.

"Everyone calm down," their father said. Romeo stepped into their midst, still casting an impressive figure at eighty-five human years. "Everyone will have their chance to say their piece about it. Meanwhile we all need to take a step back. There are men, men we've known in our pack for generations, who've just lost everything that was dear to them. They easily cut our numbers and our hearts, so we need to take some time to grieve. Then, we need to execute a plan of attack that will wipe this blight from the face of the earth and I have an idea on how to do it."

"You can't be serious," Sarina said, pacing again, which she did whenever she was aggravated or irritated about something. "This is lunacy."

"Do you have any other suggestions?" Brody asked, earning him a not so pleasant look from his mate. "I understand how uncomfortable this is for you."

"You don't," she said angrily. "None of you know how painful this would be for me, or you wouldn't have asked in the first place."

"Sarina," Romeo said, stopping when he saw the pain and hurt in her eyes. "I'm sorry, sweetheart. We know it's unfair to ask this of you, but without this important link, we may never best Fenris and his attacks on our people will continue."

"So sending me to the slaughter is the best and only alternative?" she countered. "Not only was I unknowingly seduced by that man, I bore the shame of carrying babies that could just have easily been his. And now my family wants me to seek him out so he can help us defeat his own pack? Do you even know how insane that sounds?"

"Forget we asked," Romeo said, meaning it. "You're right. We'll have to find another way to get this done."

When her relatives had left, Sarina started to head upstairs when she heard Brody say, "You could have been more help back there."

"What?"

"All I'm saying is that you could have been more help. You could have offered another alternative if you weren't up for finding Brandt."

"Seriously?" she asked, her heart already bruised, was now breaking. "You of all people should know what it was like for me and yet you'll stand there and tell me I haven't done enough?"

"I just think you had more to say," Brody said, walking past her. Sarina stalked to their room and let the tears fall as she went. What the hell was happening to her life? How had things gone from blissfully happy to this? Checking on the boys to make sure they were sleeping, Sarina drew herself a bath and sank into the heat, hoping it'd give her a little perspective on the entire ordeal.

She could understand the plight of the men who'd lost their families. She knew she wouldn't be able to cope much either if it'd had been Brody and the boys who'd been murdered. Still, she thought what her father had suggested went too far. How could anyone expect her to face the man who'd taken advantage of her in such a terrible way?

After a long soak, Sarina stepped out and heard Brody Jr. and Jedidiah start to fuss. Their cries picked up in intensity as she dressed and by the time she was able to get to them, they were screaming. "Hey," she cooed. "Mama's here. I've got you." She nursed and rocked them back to sleep, placing them together on her bed, before she went to find Brody. Her concern peaked when he wasn't anywhere in the house to be found.

Lately, his episodes had been happening more and more as she found herself slowly being pushed away. She hadn't talked to her mother about it, for fear of stirring up a hornet's nest that wasn't really there. Now though, she knew something was seriously wrong. Bundling up the boys, she drove to her mother's home to discuss bad news for the second time in as many days.

"Hi, Honey," Amanda said in greeting.

"Hey," she said, sticking her head in the backseat to undo the twins. Picking up a carrier, she was relieved when her mother took the other one.

"Everything okay? You look perplexed."

"I'm worried about Brody," Sarina said.

"What's the matter with my munchkin?" Amanda asked, looking at the baby in the carrier she held.

"Not little Brody Jr., big Brody. I took a bath after the boys fell asleep and when I got out, the boys were crying and he wasn't anywhere to be found."

"He didn't leave a note?"

"No note, no goodbye, no anything. We argued after everyone left this afternoon. I was irritated and didn't want to talk about it, so I drew myself a bath. When I got out that was when I noticed he wasn't there."

"How'd the poultice I gave him work out?"

"I'm not sure it did, to be honest," Sarina said with a sigh of defeat. "I don't know what's going on with him, but something has changed him. He's not the man I've known from the beginning, Mama."

"Well, people do change over time, but not drastically usually, at least not so drastically over such a short time. He said he didn't come into contact with anything that might have caused this issue, but I'm not so sure anymore. Somehow, whoever or whatever is affecting him had to have touched him somehow," said Amanda.

"He killed Fenris' magician, Mama. I would think that someone studying the black magic would have some dark things in their soul."

"That's true," Amanda replied. "You're sure Brody killed him?"

"He was in his wolf, but yes I'm sure."

"Good," Amanda said. "That at least gives me something to go on."

"Can you watch the boys for me? I'm going to do as Daddy suggested. If my reaching out to Brandt can bring a resolution to this whole thing, than I owe it to our pack to try."

"I admire you," Amanda said, giving Sarina's hand a squeeze. "Not every woman could do what you're doing."

"I don't doubt it," Sarina said, giving her mom a half-hearted smile. "I'll be back as soon as possible, but I'm not sure when that'll be."

"Jason's going with you," Amanda said in such a motherly tone that Sarina didn't argue. "He'll also help you find Brody. If what you're saying is what I think it is, he'll need us."

Chapter Ten

Brody came to in the woods, his clothes were the same as they had been the afternoon before when he'd… when he'd argued with Sarina. *What the hell had gotten into him?* Recalling the argument, he couldn't believe he'd stood there and berated her about not hunting down the man who'd tricked her into sleeping with him, not once, but twice. Not to mention, this same man had purposefully tried to impregnate his Sarina in hopes of holding the children over her head so she'd do what he wanted.

Looking around, he noticed that night had fallen, making the woods an eerie place to be. Fog covered the ground so that wisps of cotton air hovered over the damp underbrush. A chill ran over his skin as the sounds of the night picked up. The thought of changing crossed his mind, but without a source of food and water, he'd be stuck as a werewolf with no clothes, especially if he needed to change back quickly.

Still, when the woman from his nightmares came walking towards him, he wasn't sure he really cared about clothes. Growling low in his throat, Brody bared his teeth, even as she pulled at his most basic sexual desires.

"So moody," she said, her face grinning as she all but glided toward him. She was tall, fitting her beautiful frame into a blood-red dress with a slit up the thigh that left an open and noticeable invitation. "I like my men moody. My dogs too, for that matter. Do you know why I chose you, Brody?"

Her accent sounded Russian in origin, although he wasn't positive. Her dark hair was nearly black, especially at night with just the moon to light his way. He could smell the perfume she'd sprayed on her body and as she drew closer, the sexual ardor she put off made it hard for him to concentrate.

"What do you want from me?" said Brody.

"Oh, well that's a loaded question for sure," she laughed. Her hand reached out and slid up his arm. "For starters, I would very much enjoy you in my bed, although I don't doubt I'd have to work a little for it. As for the rest, you'll learn in time. I want to thank you for entertaining me in your mind."

"Did I have a choice?" Brody snapped, only to have her nails rake over his skin, slicing his flesh open. Cursing, he stripped a piece of his shirt off and tied it around the wounds. "You're a mad woman."

"No," she smiled. "I'm not mad in the least. In fact, I'm rather very giddy. You've given me life again and for that I am extremely grateful."

"What do you mean, *given you life again?*"

"I was killed a while back... some very bad dealings, trust me. Ever since then I've been looking for a way back and you gave me one. It was quite the undertaking and thanks to Dankar and Fenris, it was made a possibility to me. You can imagine my shock when I ended up in your mind. I do like a playground though and you gave me a fascinating one. You have some serious pent up sexual energy buzzing around in there, especially for the woman who must be your mate."

"Don't touch her," Brody said, earning him a solid slap to his face.

"You don't rule here, dog. You'll be smart to remember that. Fenris, my lover, doesn't even rule here, despite the reprieve I've had to have."

"You're Lilith," Brody said, remembering the stories he'd heard from Romeo and Amanda about the woman who'd sided with Penelope's uncle to try and steal Amanda's powers. Apparently to hear him tell it, she was also quite infatuated with Romeo.

"So, someone's been telling stories. Why don't you tell me what you know?"

When Brody resisted, she upped the pain by breaking his thumbs.

"Now, how about we start again. It's been quite a while since I've been in the loop on things here. Tell me about Romeo and his whore. Surely they've started a family, lived their lives. I want to know everything."

"Go to hell," Brody growled.

"Oh, honey. I've already been there," said Lilith, smiling. Her hand, impossibly strong, squeezed his windpipe so that he couldn't breathe. "Now, I won't ask again. Fail to answer me this time and I'll simply snap your neck and leave you where you lie. There are plenty of dogs around here who will tell me what I want to know for far less hassle."

Sarina and the twins flashed through Brody's mind. They'd be defenseless if she killed him. Reluctantly, Brody told her what he knew, keeping things as vague as possible. "Romeo married Amanda Walker-Traverse and they have five children. Two sets of twins and a son in the middle. They live in Mabel Traverse's mansion that she left to Amanda upon her death. They've been attacked by Fenris."

"Well, well. My little pup got busy while I was gone. I'll have to make him pay for that," she grinned. "Now, where is Fenris?"

"The last I knew, he'd left his caves, which are far to the Northwest of us."

"Excellent," she said, smiling. "I should tell you that when I finally free you, you're going to be freezing cold. The temperature dropped drastically last night and without me inside of you, you'll be subjected to the harsh elements. I want to say before I go though, that it was most enjoyable being inside your head. You have some interesting fantasies in there. You should tell your mate… she may be more into them than you think."

"Wait!" Brody shouted, only to find himself alone in the pitch black of the woods, his body already shaking from hypothermia.

"You're sure he went this way?" Jason asked, walking with his sister.

"No," she said. "I'm sure that he's been screwed up since he killed that black magician Fenris had working for him. That's what I know. I know that somewhere out here my mate is in trouble. I can feel it."

"Alright," Jason said, holding his hands up. "I'm not trying to be a dick. I'm just trying to help."

"I know," Sarina sighed. "Thank you for coming along. I appreciate the company."

"I wouldn't leave you to do this alone," Jason said, touching her arm. "No matter how much I bitch when we're home."

Sarina looked at her twin then and knew that no matter what, he'd always have her back. "When did you grow up?"

"Sometime last week," he grinned. "I think I found my mate."

"Seriously?"

"You remember Patricia Cursey?"

"The little fiery red head from school?"

"Yeah. She came into her breeding season this year. She flew under my radar forever, until I stopped by the café a couple weeks ago. She was waitressing and I sat in her section. Wow, is all I have to say about her. She took my breath away and I haven't gotten it back yet."

"Does she know how you feel?"

"Pretty sure she does," Jason smiled.

"Christ almighty," Sarina moaned. "We have to stay chaste as if our lives depended on it and you get to gallivant all over creation, screwing whoever you like."

"Gallivant? Who even says that anymore?"

"Screw you Jay. I'm a mother. I have to sound smart."

"My nephews are in trouble already," Jason laughed. Then he stuck an arm out, stopping Sarina in her tracks.

"What is it?"

"I don't know, but whatever it is, it's not good. Can't you feel that… that darkness?"

"No," Sarina said.

"It's tugging at me, like… like liquid sex."

"Jesus—"

"I'm serious," Jason said, his eyes widening.

"Tell me more," Sarina said.

"It's feral, all heat and action. There's absolutely nothing soft in it. It's female in nature and whoever she is, she wants nothing soft in return. No romance for her. She's seeking someone, someone like me, but different."

"Hello, Romeo," came a sultry voice from the darkness.

"I'm not Romeo," Jason answered. "He's my father, but if I can help you in some way…"

"Oh, yes, I see now." The disembodied voice was louder now.

Jason and Sarina watched a beautifully stunning woman step out into the light of the moon. "You have the look of your father. All brawn, very little brains. Who is the little tramp with you?"

"She's not a tramp. She's my twin, Sarina."

"So, my little mongrel was telling me the truth."

"You're *her*," Sarina said, her body starting the change she hadn't attempted in months, let alone without the full moon. Suddenly her body contorted in breath stealing pain as the woman lifted her into the air.

"Don't even think about it girl," the woman seethed. "Unless you want your mate to die in these woods. Put your wolf away or I'll do it for you."

When she was dropped back to the forest floor, Sarina whimpered as she became her human self again. "What do you want with us?"

"I want nothing to do with you," she spat at Sarina. "You, on the other hand," she purred at Jason, winding her body around him in a blatantly sexual move. Her hand reached for his crotch, rubbing against his already bulging cock. "You and I could find some time to enjoy each other. You do look so much like your father. Tell me, do you rule like him as well?"

"My father still rules," Jason said, his hand sliding up to cup the woman's breast. "I won't take over the Delta pack, until he chooses to step down."

"What if he's disgraced and forced out?" she purred, her tongue darting into his ear.

"There's nothing that can disgrace my father," he said with a grin. "He's the best alpha I've ever known."

Sarina watched their interplay with a sick feeling in the pit of her stomach. "Jason, we need to find Brody and get him back home before Mom and Dad start to worry."

"Now, now," the woman groaned. "Why don't you go find Brody and let your brother stay here with me? I've got things to do that he can be a great help to me with."

When Sarina took Jason's hand, she found herself hurling through the woods, her body slamming hard against a tall, thick spruce tree. The woman was standing in front of her within seconds, "I said to go find your dog. I'll see that your brother makes it home just fine."

"I won't leave him," Sarina moaned, her body fighting to stand.

"Then you'll foolishly waste your life here," the woman said, grabbing Sarina's windpipe and squeezing it.

<<◇>>

Brody could feel Sarina choking, as if she was inside his body. Unlike the woman who'd been inside his head, this was a sort of out of body experience. He'd changed into his wolf the moment the woman left him to ward off the freezing wind and was now close to the border where the woods ran into Delta pack territory.

Racing toward the feeling, Brody saw them with his eyes first. The woman was holding Sarina, who looked pretty mangled, in the air, her hand around his mate's windpipe. Jason, who had also changed, was charging the woman, his growl echoing in the distance. Brody watched the woman catch Jason in midair and snap his neck, dropping his body where it landed. Already in midair his own self, Brody was unable to stop his momentum and slammed into the woman, knocking her back. Standing guard over Sarina, who was weeping silently under his large body, Brody growled at the woman.

"Well, well," the woman smirked. "Aren't you the protective one? Perhaps I was too hasty in sending you on your way. Would you like to come back to me?"

His growl intensified, but he stayed where he was,
until the woman simply turned and walked away.
Turning, he changed, kneeling by Sarina, whose
weeping turned to sobs that wracked her body. Jason
lay in the grass, his body having changed back to that of
a man. Brody piled leaves up to cover his nakedness
and sat holding the woman who'd been closest to him.

"We need to get you both home," Brody said after
nearly two hours of waiting. His heart hurt for her, but
he knew sitting here would do little to solve anyone's
problems. Standing, Brody helped Sarina to her feet and
then stooped to pick up Jason's body.

As soon as they made it to the Traverse mansion,
Brody watched Amanda step off the porch and crumple
to the ground, Romeo and Sarina's other siblings
coming slowly out as well. It took everyone close to
two hours to get Sarina and Amanda to lie down.
Shawna, Sarina's younger sister, made a poultice for
Sarina's throat, which she spread over her once she'd
fallen asleep.

"Tell me everything," Romeo demanded.

"It was Lilith," Brody said, rushing to explain. "I
know you killed her here, but she found a way to come
back. Apparently, from what she said, she'd been
working with Dankar for years to find a portal to come
back. When I killed him, I became her portal. She used
my mind and body to move from the depths of hell to
Earth. Sarina wouldn't leave Jason once Lilith found
them. She wanted to do more with Jason than he would
have wanted and Sarina wouldn't leave him. So Lilith

started choking her. Jason changed and charged her. She just reached out, caught him in midair and snapped his neck. I've never seen anyone do anything like that, especially to a beta wolf. I was already in the air and thankfully I knocked her away from Sarina. She wouldn't fight me as a wolf and finally left. It took me hours to get Sarina up and moving so we could bring Jason home."

"That bitch will pay for this," Romeo said, his own emotions coming to the surface. "There is no other alpha to take my place now. Wade is an Omega and Joshua is too young, even if he were to come into alpha powers. I'm afraid she has done what Fenris only dreamed of doing. The Traverse alpha line died with Jason."

"What about Sarina?" Brody asked. "She is as much alpha material as Jason was."

"She's a breeder," Romeo said, as if that ended the conversation.

"She's more than that," Brody argued. "She can and will lead when given the opportunity."

"She ran off and mated with you after two days. She got kidnapped twice, and she nearly died tonight."

Frustrated, Brody added, "Jason did none of those things and he did *die* tonight. Mistakes don't make a bad leader. Not owning up to them makes a bad leader."

"Don't you dare speak of my son as if you knew him," Romeo growled. "Just because you seduced my daughter and mated with her, doesn't make you family."

Brody couldn't have been more hurt if someone had snapped his neck that night. Angry, he left the mansion, taking his sons with him and headed home. He knew Sarina would rest well there and he'd see about her recovery in the morning. Tonight he needed the solace and isolated quiet of their home. He tucked the twins into his bed and sat in the rocker recliner, thinking.

Chapter Eleven

Fenris sat in his chair just staring. He was speechless, well beyond words as he stared at the woman in front of him. Beyond stunning, she was the woman of his dreams, the Lilith he remembered from his youth. "How?"

"Oh, darling," she purred. "It'd take much too long to tell. I'm famished and exhausted. Feed me and find me a bed."

Fenris did as she asked, finding her the most succulent meal they could prepare. He took it to her in his own quarters. "I'm sorry I don't currently have anything better."

"Do not worry, darling," she said, grinning. "I have a feeling you'll be seeing a war on your lawn before you know it."

His growl of approval made her smile, but when he made an advance at her, she laughed. "Please, Fenris," she said. "It's been nearly five hundred years. Look at you. While I will always love you, there is nothing between us any longer. I will have Romeo Traverse in my bed, or I will die again, trying."

"Traverse is nothing but a wet dog. He couldn't please you if he tried, which I doubt he'd be inclined to do, if what you say is true."

"Not only is it true," Lilith smiled, "I'll take down everyone he loves until he comes to me willingly."

"Careful," Fenris warned. "I had his daughter and her twins in my clutches and not only did he rescue them, he took out six of my best wolves."

"Ah, Fenris," she said. "You were always too soft. The difference between you and me is that I wouldn't have kept her. I'd have cut the children from her and killed them all on the spot, for that is how you start a war."

"Starting a war isn't my issue. I was well on my way, not that I'm complaining about your contribution. If they were going to take their time with things and try to get around me, your little tactic will surely up their enthusiasm for a good, bloody fight."

"There's no rush. We want them to scatter and be emotional. The more, the better. Emotions don't belong in war and when they come, if their emotions are high, they'll mess up. That's all the better for us. Now, I'm tired and want my peace. Leave me be for now. In the morning we'll talk again."

Fenris once again did as Lilith asked, but he didn't rest himself. He was pent up, frustrated by her refusal. He knew he'd aged a bit since they were last together, but they had once been inseparable lovers. Had things really changed that much? Needing the release, Fenris found the young females of his pack and took one of them by the hand. "Come with me," he said.

She was dark haired, like Lilith, and sported a figure much like that of his former lover. "I am not in season yet," the young girl said.

"It's of no matter to me," Fenris said. "I'm not looking to mate, nor to breed."

"Oh."

"Is this your first time?"

"No," the girl blushed.

"Good," Fenris growled. He took her ruthlessly with little care for her comfort or enjoyment. When he was finished, he dismissed her, giving her twenty-four hours to herself. Then he collapsed in his bed and brooded over the dark haired beauty who'd rebuffed his attention.

Brandt couldn't believe how his life had changed. He'd gone from a womanizing ass, to a stable, soon-to-be father all in less than four months. Apparently Fenris hadn't cared much that he'd never returned. Either that or the old wolf was losing his touch. Frankly he couldn't have cared less either way.

Life with Carly was amazing. She was carrying their child well and seemed to be in her element in the small cabin. Brandt never would have admitted to wanting children. Having Carly for a mate had been his way out of all of that mess, but when she'd told him she was pregnant, he'd discovered a protective side to himself he'd never really known before. Now, he knew he'd do anything in his power to make sure both she and the baby stayed healthy so she could carry this one to term, whatever that meant for a werewolf. He'd finished the addition just in time for the colder weather and Carly had worked hard to turn it into a bedroom, saving the smaller room for storage, not that they had much to store. Brandt knew that showing his face in town was risky, even if he'd been Brody the last few times he'd been there. Any chance that someone might recognize him was too much chance. He couldn't ask Carly to go either, not with her pregnancy progressing so quickly.

There was a part of him that sometimes thought about how things would have been different if he hadn't found Carly that night, or if one of the Duscene twins had been his. Seeing Carly, hugely pregnant with his child, made him wonder what it'd be like to hold his child in his arms, to feel swamped by parental love.

"You're brooding again," Carly said as she stepped out of the cabin to find him.

"Just thinking about life," he replied, taking her outstretched hand and pulling her close. He wrapped his arms around her middle and sighed when he felt the baby kick. "How are you feeling?"

"Huge and tired. The baby seems more restless than usual."

"Maybe your time is closer than we thought?"

"I don't see how, although this is the first baby I've ever carried this far. He seems to be growing fast, much faster than a normal human baby anyway. I'm not sure any of this is normal."

From out of nowhere, a voice spoke up. "Werewolf babies are often much faster growers than our fully human counterparts."

Startled, both Brandt and Carly turned to see the woman who'd spoken.

"Sarina?" Brandt said in disbelief. "How'd you find me?"

"Not as easily as you found me," she said. "I've run across this cabin before. There was a woman who used to live here. I suppose she's gone now. Anyway I'll make this quick as it's uncomfortable for everyone. I need… rather, my pack needs your help. We need to know where Fenris is… what his plans are before we eliminate him from the world."

"I have no idea where he is. I haven't been in the caves in over four months. Fenris gave me a twenty-four hour leave after I brought you there. I never went back after that."

"Why?"

"Carly was waiting for me," he said, motioning toward his pregnant mate. "I can't say I've turned my life around really, but I hope to stay out of whatever issues your pack has with Fenris."

"Now you want to stay out of it? You all but started this shit and now you want to opt out as if you were just an innocent bystander?"

"I know what I did was wrong. I know that I can't ever make it up to you, but I don't want to take your side either."

"You arrogant son-of-a-bitch!" Sarina yelled. "You're nothing but a pussy. I've seen cowards in my day, but you are the epitome of the word."

"Say whatever you want," Brandt said. "But with Carly expecting, I can't leave her. We're not exactly in the state to just rush her to the hospital when her time comes."

"My mother had me and my brother at home. I would have had my twins at home if you'd left well enough alone," Sarina started. "Carly is capable of handling one baby here. Do you have the things you need?"

What the hell had gotten into her? Here she was, offering to help the man who'd seduced and abducted her, get ready for his child to be born. Hadn't she just told him what a bastard he was? Sighing, Sarina moved first, stepping into their cabin without asking permission.

"You need much more firewood," she said, looking at the pile they had inside. "You need blankets and clothing. Haven't you thought about anything?"

"We weren't sure what to get," the woman said. Sarina looked at her then. She was petite, her mating mark clearly visible. Sarina shut down the nosy part of her that wanted to pry into their relationship. What sort of woman mated with a man who'd do what Brandt did? Shaking her head as if to clear it, she made a list and handed it to Brandt. "These are the things you need."

"We have no money," he said, looking very much like a petulant child. Reaching into her back pocket, Sarina pulled out her wallet and slapped down a wad of cash.

"Use this," she said. "If you need more, come see me. You should know where I live." At least he had the decency to look sorrowful over the entire ordeal. "When her time comes, keep the house warm, maybe even overly warm. Our babies tend to grow fast and deliver fast. Make sure the sheets and blankets are ready and if you think you can get word to me, do it. I'll come help."

Without another word, Sarina stepped back outside and started to walk away from the cabin. "Sarina, wait!"

She turned, seeing Brandt coming toward her. She leaned to the left slightly to see Carly standing on the small stoop. "Yeah?"

"Look, I… I know it doesn't change anything, but I wanted to say I'm sorry for what I did to you, how I used you. I had no right to do what I did and having Carly in my life now helped me realize that if anyone ever did to her what I did to you, I'd kill him. Thank you for not sending your husband after me."

"He's not my husband," Sarina said, obviously still irritated. "But I'll tell him. All's well that ends well." She didn't reach out and touch him, but she gave him a half smile before she turned around and left.

By the time she got home, Brody looked as if he'd lost his mind. The house was a mess and the twins were sleeping on what looked to be a pallet that had been made up on the floor. He was sitting on the couch, staring at the TV. "Hey," he said. "How are you feeling?"

"Tired, emotionally exhausted, rundown. You?"

"The same, pretty much," he answered. "Wanna help me get these two up to bed?"

"Sure," she said with a grin and looking at her sons. Nearly five months old, they were starting to show the differences in their personalities. Brody Jr. was rambunctious and always going. Jedidiah on the other hand was quieter, more reserved and introverted. It'd be quite the privilege to watch them continue to grow into young men.

Brody picked up Jedidiah and Sarina took Brody Jr., laying them side-by-side in their bed.

"We're never getting this back, you know," said Brody.

"I know," she sighed. "The time goes by so quickly."

"I sort of meant, our bed," he said, grinning.

"Oh," she laughed. "That I don't mind sacrificing."

"Speak for yourself," he grumbled. "I haven't slept next to my wife in what feels like months."

"At the rate we were going, I wasn't sure you really cared to be with me, let alone sleep next to me."

"You know that wasn't me, right?"

"Sure the hell felt like you," she said, her bright green eyes looking straight into his.

Brody realized then just how much he'd damaged their relationship, just how much he'd hurt her. It wasn't enough to gloss over it as if it'd never happened.

"Come here," he said, holding out his hand.

When she took it, he led her to their spare bathroom. He cranked the shower on and adjusted the water temperature to the setting she liked and then came back to her, slowly undressing her. She still sported the nasty bruising around her throat from where Lilith had choked her, but only now was he finding all the bruising that ran over her back and ribs from hitting the tree when she'd been tossed through the air.

"I'm going to kill her," Brody said, laying a gentle hand against her back. The bruising ran down onto her buttocks and spread over her ribs and collarbone. When she was naked, he held the shower door open.

"Come on," he said.

"Thank you," she said with a sigh.

Brody felt her press a kiss to his cheek before she stepped into the heat. She just stood there letting the water pour over her hair, turning her dark tresses nearly black. Blood, from a head wound she hadn't mentioned, pooled around her feet and washed down the drain. Brody just sat back and watched her soak her body forever, letting the heat undo the tension, stress, fear, and uncertainty of life. When she seemed visibly relaxed, Brody stripped and silently joined her in their two person shower stall. He slid his hand gently over hers before she could turn off the water. "Not all of us are done just yet." She stood up and turned to face him, her body making him ache despite the bruises that were just beginning to heal.

Brody fought the urge to touch her, knowing if he did, he'd push her for more than she was ready to give. She needed to learn to separate him from the man he'd been when Lilith was pushing him. "I love you," he said, needing her to know it, even if she didn't believe him.

"I know," she said, cupping his cheek in her hand. She stepped from the shower and Brody didn't stop her. Sighing with relief, he showered himself, toweling off and pulling on boxers and the pajama bottoms she'd just bought him before the twins came along. Shutting off the light to the bathroom, Brody headed out through the guest room and nearly ran right over Sarina, who'd been waiting for him in the doorway.

"Sarina?" he said, gripping her arms to keep from knocking her over. The light from the hallway did little to illuminate Sarina's face, but Brody felt the warmth of her breath on his cheek.

"Take me," she whispered. Closing his eyes, Brody bit his tongue. What the hell was a man to do when the woman he loved was asking him to have her? Before he could even try to object she added, "Please."

Chuckling softly Brody pressed his brow to hers. "Oh, Love. You have no idea what it's like for me right now. I want you so bad I can practically combust just thinking about it. But would I really be giving you what you need? Do you even trust me?"

That was the crux of his issue, Brody knew. He had no way of knowing whether Sarina trusted that it was truly him, that he loved her more than anything. Then her slender fingers touched his face and that wonderful mouth pressed against his. A better man may have tried to push her back and give her time, but Brody had gone weeks - months since the twins' birth - without so much as a whisper of sex with his mate.

Taking her hands, Brody led her back into the spare bedroom, having her sit on the bed. "Do your bruises hurt?"

"Some, but not terribly," she replied. Knowing then the need for his own sacrifice, Brody kissed her long and deep, slowly turning her on with the slide of his tongue over hers. He touched her body just as slowly, his hands gentle even as they worked to arouse her. Brody kissed her everywhere, spending ample time on her beautiful full breasts. He kneaded them softly, not wanting to squirt himself with milk.

Continuing to kiss her, Brody slipped two fingers into the wet heat he found at her center, enjoying the way she moaned and let her hips buck against him. Shifting his body, Brody moved easily between her open thighs and smiled when his tongue flicked over her clit. Her excited gasp only encouraged him to take her slowly this way. His tongue slid slowly over her already swollen folds, tasting her arousal. He showered her clit with attention, running slow circles over and around it, as his fingers continued to fill her. His own body screamed for release as Brody showed Sarina undivided attention. She came with a cry of his name, her hands buried in his hair. Just as he went to move from her though, he felt her hands tug on him. "Please take me now," she quietly asked.

Undone by her, Brody came back to her, settling himself between her inviting hips. He kissed her fully, feeling her arousal against the tip of his cock. On a sigh, he sank into her. Her ripe pussy fed his need as he worked to make her orgasm again. Brody felt the ridges of her hot snatch all but suck him in with each thrust, pushing him harder toward his own climax. His hands ran up her thigh, pulling her leg higher so that each of his thrusts went deeper and deeper still. Unable to control his own passion, Brody pushed both of Sarina's legs toward her chest, his cock filling her as fully as he could until her orgasm clamped around him and yanked him over that hard, full edge. Filling her again, Brody spilled his essence deep into her warm pussy before he rolled over, collapsing on their spare bed.

Chapter Twelve

They spent half an hour holding each other afterward, before Sarina got up to check on the twins, who slept peacefully. When Brody joined her, they climbed into bed and slept with their sons.

The next morning, Sarina and Brody showered and dressed before dressing the twins and placing them in their car seats for the trip to her parent's home. Today they'd say goodbye to Jason and bury him in the family plot next to Sarina's great Aunt Mabel who'd been buried there more than twenty-five years prior.

Sarina found her sister, Shawna, and together the women held each other as the grief for their lost brother overwhelmed them. Sarina waited for Brody to join them with the twins and together the five of them headed into the house where Sarina found her parents. Her mother still looked shell shocked, her dark eyes holding none of the happiness she'd been so well known for. "Mama," Sarina said, placing her arms around her mother's waist. Her mother grabbed her tight, holding her for a long time.

"We need to get started," Joshua said, seeming so much older to Sarina now. Her grandfather was the rock that held their family together and Sarina didn't want to think about what they'd all do when he left this world.

"Thank you all for coming today," Romeo said, standing near the place where Jason's body had been placed. "Today is a day no parent should have to live through, the burying of a child. Jason Jeremiah Traverse was a prankster and fiercely competitive, especially with his twin sister, Sarina. No one loved his family with more openness than Jason though and I stand here today knowing that somewhere out there, he's enjoying himself. That was Jason's legacy, because no matter how bad things got, no matter how much trouble he got into, he always, always found the positive in it. He always found a way to entertain people and lived to make people smile."

Sarina spoke of Jason's love for his pack, his dreams and fears of taking the alpha position when Romeo stepped down. She told stories from their childhood and promised not only that she'd never forget him, but that she'd end those responsible for his death. Then she stepped away and joined Brody and her sons, who looked like serious little toddlers in their tiny suits.

Fenris watched the funeral from a short distance away. He'd needed confirmation that Lilith wasn't just jerking his chain and sending a recruit wasn't good enough. Still, seeing the Delta pack mourning the loss of a wolf, even an important one, was so much fun. His pack knew they'd better damn well do their grieving in private and get it over with. No one was important in his pack and any grieving that had to be done was set aside until the main objective was taken care of. He needed soldiers and warriors, not sniveling little bitches and bastards.

It was even more obvious to him now that the Delta pack needed a leader who'd turn them into the werewolves they were meant to be. They were hybrids after all. The last thing they needed was to walk around acting like their weak and needy, human counterparts. Humans were prey and it was time someone reminded the Delta pack of that fact, among many others.

He returned to his base, noticing the changes that had occurred since his leaving that morning. "What the hell is all this?"

"It's management," Lilith said, her body decked out in tight jeans and a tank top. Growling, he took her arm and all but yanked her into his conference room.

"You of all people don't come into my domain and try to take over. I'm the alpha now Lilith, as I remember you died a quarter of a century ago by caring too much for a particular weak link in my rather impressive line."

"And what's more impressive? The fact that I came back from the dead or that you're still alive? I'm the one who started this line, or do I need to remind you?"

"I don't need a reminder, you little bitch. If it wasn't for you, I'd have had some fun with you and gone about my merry way. Do you have any idea what that first change was like for me? I felt as if I was dying, except I never got that release. I never died… I just suffered, trying to grasp what was happening to me.”

“Poor baby,” Lilith said, mocking him.

Fenris pinned her against the wall, devouring her body with his eyes.

“What aggravates you more? The fact that I started actually doing something here, or that I won’t let you have me?” she asked.

“You never could take orders well,” Fenris said. Reaching up, he tore her shirt away, exposing the sloping curve of her breasts. Dipping his head, he ran his tongue over her flesh, his keen ears picking up the way she gasped. “The hell you don’t want me.”

One sharp look into her eyes and Fenris fused his mouth to hers, inhaling her scent as his hands worked her clothes off. Their mating was fast and rough, each taking exactly what they wanted from the other. When all was said and done, Fenris sat back and grinned. “It’s been too long, Lilith.”

“Hmm,” she mumbled. Looking at the white board across the room, she went over to it and began to draw in large sweeping lines. “You need more soldiers. The Delta pack easily outnumbers your forces. Even with the blow to their lines last week and the devastation I caused by taking out their alpha’s son, we’re going to need more wolves.”

“And where exactly do you expect to find them? That little whelp went and submitted his pack to Romeo months ago, they're certainly not going to be a big help. Other packs, who knows what they have going, not to mention the cost of traveling to them and then trying to convince them that this is best. What the hell can we offer them for their time and sacrifice?"

"How about becoming a member of the strongest and most notorious pack this side of the River? No pack is going to best ours once we join with the Delta wolves. Our forces will be unstoppable and instead of living in damp, dark caves, we'll ride high in that mansion Romeo and his bitch have."

"Lilith, I love your grandiose schemes, but I'm not sure that asking other packs to join us in hopes of taking down the Delta pack and joining us all together is going to be enough to convince them to fight."

"Well, then," Lilith smiled. "We'll have to make a reason for them to want to participate. Something along the lines of sabotage caused by none other than the Delta pack. All we have to do is figure out how they kill and leave a few werewolf bodies around for pack members to find. They'll trace those kills back here and before you know it, we'll have ourselves an army to take down Romeo, his bitch, their mongrel pups and anyone else who thinks they can stand in our way."

Smiling, Fenris agreed that her plan was a solid one. He wasn't sure it'd go off all that smoothly, but if they could nail the execution, he believed they'd definitely have themselves an army that not even Romeo's best wolves could beat. His body finally sated by taking

Lilith, Fenris called several of his best to a conference and explained Lilith's initial phase to them.

"Report back to me when it's done," he said, releasing them to go. He knew waiting would be the hardest part, but within the week, they'd hear something from the other packs for certain, especially when they came sweeping over the mountains to find the pack responsible for killing off their members. Boy, wasn't Romeo's pack going to be in for a surprise.

Looking over at Lilith, Fenris was surprised to see her staring at him, her face curiously blank for a minute. Then those eyes he'd always loved smiled at him. "Come to my quarters later. It's been a hell of a trip back and you've whetted my appetite for carnal pleasures."

Fenris gave her a simple shake of his head to voice his agreement and when she left he spent some time thinking of the maneuvers they'd put into place. It was good, solid strategy, but they'd need to be two steps ahead to make it all work. Come morning, he'd talk with his pack about it. Right now though, he had a woman to please and pleasure of his own to take.

-To be continued in Book 3-

If you enjoyed this title, I would appreciate your leaving a review of the book. Good reviews encourage an author to write as well as help books to sell. Good reviews can be just a few short sentences describing what you liked about the book without having a spoiler.

If you could spend 30 seconds writing a review, I would appreciate it: you can review this title right now at your favorite retailer.

Here is a preview of the **next story** you may enjoy:

Alpha Bait: Romeo Alpha Blood Lines Romance, Book 3

SARINA TRAVERSE sat in her mother's living room perusing wedding magazines. As the oldest of the Walker-Traverse children, she felt a certain responsibility to throw a party no one would forget for some time to come. At least until Shawna married. The boys, Wade and Joshua wouldn't care one way or another when it was their turn to marry. Sucking in her lip she tried to stem the tears that still wanted to fall at the thought of her twin, Jason.

It had been nearly three months since he'd been killed by Lilith, the once dead and now reliving creator of the werewolf and initial maker of both of Fenris' packs. The Delta pack had risen, thanks in huge part to the Traverse clan, all the way back past Sarina's grandfather, Jeremiah. Romeo, Sarina's father, had worked hard, struggled and sacrificed to keep a peace between the Delta pack and other outlying packs. Some had even submitted their alpha position and joined themselves with the Delta pack, becoming a large family of werewolves who looked out for one another.

Sarina had been so excited to turn twenty-four, to do her part in keeping the Delta pack strong. Then she'd met her now mate, Brody. He was the father of her twin boys, Jedidiah and Brody Jr., who were just about to start walking and were already well on their way to forming sentences. Apparently growing quickly wasn't just a phenomenon that affected them in the womb, but for the whole of their lives, at least until the change came. She was grateful she had another ten to twelve years before that happened.

"He would have loved seeing them," Sarina said, her heart still broken. "Jason would have been the best uncle."

"Yes he would have," Amanda Traverse said softly. Since losing her son, Amanda had barely spoken. The first weeks after his death, she'd barely eaten enough to stay alive, so lost in her grief that she truly didn't care at the time whether or not she lived. Now, while she still wasn't herself, probably never truly would be again, she at least ate and conversed some. "Judging by his first change, you'd have a disgruntled opinion of your brother as uncle material. Jason was a little hellion during his first shift. Couldn't blame him though, it's a painful and overwhelming process."

"Sort of like our first breeding, huh?" said Sarina.

"A lot like it yes, but different, in so many ways. Our shift comes because we want it to. Our men shift whether they want to or not. Every full moon, they morph into werewolves and stalk into the brush and woods to find prey. Don't forget, my daughter. No one asks for this life. I found out at twenty-four what my parents were, who I was. It took me several more years to truly come to grips with the reality of it. Even after I'd married your father and had you and Jason."

"Was it difficult, learning all of that literally overnight?"

She knew she'd heard the stories a million times since she was little, but listening to them always soothed her soul and Sarina hoped they'd take her mother to a happier time. Anything to pull her from the loss of one of her children.

"Your father was like a handsome ogre. He was an overbearing ass who thought everything was his way or the highway. I just had to show him that compromise was definitely in his best interest." Sarina caught the hint of a smile on her mother's lips before her eyes dulled again. Moving closer, Sarina wrapped her arms around her mother, pulling her close.

"Tell me more?"

Amanda hugged her back. "It didn't take long for me to realize that I'd fallen head over heels for your father, not that he'd have had it any other way, peeping Tom. Still, I wasn't about to make it easy on him. I fought him tooth and nail for every inch of freedom. I stepped into the cabin Wade has now and your father acted as if I was the Holy Grail. Wouldn't let me have a moment's peace and quiet. After we found out that you and Jason were coming it was worse, except that I was halfway around the world. I couldn't reach your father at all and he was being tortured by Remus, your Aunt Audri's first love. Things got really complicated when my half-brother Dean came into the picture, trying to steal the Radiant powers my mother had given me. That's when I met your Aunt Penelope. She was so timid. I learned early in those first conversations that this was more to ensure her safety and the secret she kept, than her actual personality."

"Aunt Pen sure has come into her own, hasn't she?"

"That she has. I, of course, fully credit her and Elijah finding their own happiness. They could have torched a house with the sparks they gave off in the beginning, even when they didn't think they could have a life together."

"Why didn't Aunt Pen just say *screw it* and become Uncle Elijah's mate anyway?"

"Because while she loved him, she loved being a Radiant, the powers her mother passed to her. She wanted to honor them to the best of her ability and she didn't think she could have both her powers and Elijah at the time."

"She's got more in her than I do," Sarina said, looking out the window.

"Your aunt would tell you that it was because she loved Elijah that she didn't throw it all away. She loved him enough to walk away from him, to let him move on, when she couldn't have him and be a Radiant. As women, particularly mothers, we have to remember that sacrificing for our families doesn't mean we give up the things we need. Your Aunt does a great job of balancing her needs and wants with those of her husband and child."

"Planning this whole thing feels sort of strange."

"Not all mates legally wed, you know?"

"I know, but after all that's happened this last year, I think both Brody and I need this. We need to know that come hell or high water, we will always choose each other, first and last. We've talked about it and in the beginning I think we sort of leaned towards not doing it, but there has been so much trying to weigh us down that we need a moment to step back, to thank everyone who's stood by and behind us in support. To say 'thank you' to everyone who's kept us safe. And who've worked to keep the boys safe."

"Any member of our pack would gladly give their lives to keep Brody Jr. and Jedidiah safe, you know that. Still, a wedding is a great way to get everyone together."

Sarina could tell that her mother was trying to be cheerful, trying hard not to let her grief show, trying hard and failing miserably at it. Still, she hoped helping with the wedding would bring a genuine smile to her face. "Why don't we plan a shopping trip?"

"Where?" asked Amanda.

"I don't know. Somewhere outside the pack. We never go outside anymore and nothing against the Delta, but we're a little behind the times and if I want a dress that's going to knock Brody off his feet, I need to look around."

"Your father isn't going to like it."

"Dad never likes anything. We're grown women. Plus, we can take Dad and Brody with us if they want to come. They can get some male bonding in over beer and pool, while we enjoy giggling like idiots over lace and tulle."

"Alright," Amanda said, the grief lifting from her eyes for a moment. "Maybe Jas…" Sarina caught the first sob from her mother before teary eyes met hers. Then her mother just turned and walked away. Her own grief was still very raw and Sarina found herself crying. She needed her twin, now more than ever. Who would be there to look after her boys when they no longer wanted their parents around? Who would teach them all the things she told them not to do? Wiping her eyes, she sniffled before she stepped out of the living room straight into her little brother, Wade. Barely more than a year behind her and Jason, he favored their father just as much as she did their mother. "Hey," he said, his voice soft, understanding. "You okay?"

"Just grieving," she said, a sheepish smile curving her lips. "How about you?"

"The same," he grinned. "Just in a different way."

"Does it help with the grief?"

"Some, but I'm not sure Brody would like you doing it."

"What is it?" asked Sarina.

"Manual labor," he said. "Actually, I'm tracking the bitch who killed Jason. No luck so far, but I'm getting closer. I can feel it."

"That whore won't know what's coming when I get my claws and teeth into her. I'll rip her throat out before she can whimper," said Sarina.

"Now there's my sister," Wade smiled. "So, if you wanna help, just let me know. I'll be heading back out in about two hours."

"Hell yes," Sarina said.

"Good. The more wolves I have looking, the sooner I'll find her trail. Do you… do you think you can show me where he… where Jason was killed?"

"Yes," Sarina said without hesitation. If it helped Wade track that spineless wench, she'd do whatever it took to avenge her brother's death. Wade looked almost relieved.

"I hate asking you, Sarina."

"I'm offering," she replied, hugging her little brother. "Besides, my helping you kick that bitch's teeth down her throat might feel a little bit like justice for Jason. Lord knows we won't be getting it any other way."

If you enjoyed this sample then look for **Alpha Bait: Romeo Alpha Blood Lines Romance, Book 3**.

Here is a preview of **another story** you may also enjoy:

Romeo Alpha: A BBW Paranormal Shifter Romance - Book 2

"**I AM** coming, my love." Amanda could hear Romeo, even though he wasn't with her. She realized that they had connected telepathically, just like he said they would, and smiled as she spoke back to him in her mind.

"I know. I am fine." She needed him to believe she was okay; even if she wasn't. She wanted to make sure he was at ease.

"I told you; no matter where you go, I will find you. I will come for you." His voice reached her ears as if he were standing in front of her, talking.

"I am coming to you."

"No, my love. I am here already."

She turned when she heard his voice. Romeo stood before her, in the middle of the field. She hadn't realized how far she had actually run. Her steps quickened the closer she got to him. He gathered her close in his arms and chuckled when she started ripping his clothes from him. He kissed her deeply and pulled her into the circle of his arms.

"We are outside, honey. Anyone could see."

"Come on, aren't you a wolf? Besides, Romeo, don't you think it is time to be ourselves?"

"You make a valid point," he said, in between kisses on her throat.

"Good, then, come on. Let's become one with nature."

He chuckled as he slowly made love to his mate there among the wild flowers and fields.

Amanda knew her work wasn't over. Somewhere out there, her brother was coming up with another plan to take her powers, but for the moment, she wanted nothing more than to feel her mate.

As Romeo slid inside her, she moaned deeply. She didn't need any foreplay or fondling. She just needed him inside her as soon as possible.

He flipped her to her hands and knees and slid inside over and over, speeding up until he was taking her with such force that she lost her balance multiple times. She reveled in it, and met him thrust for thrust, until they both screamed in pleasure.

As they lay in each other's arms afterward, they planned their next step in life and as a couple. They planned their eternity together.

It had been a month since the fiasco of Amanda's kidnapping. Amanda had decided to move into her aunt's estate with Romeo, and they were to be formally married in just two weeks' time. Her powers were growing, and she was grateful for Penelope, who came and helped her to control them. Penelope, Audri and Aurora were like the sisters she had never had, and she found herself becoming very close with them all.

Amanda began to notice that Penelope acted a little strange whenever they came around Elijah, though. Being the quiet one, he often stood aloof when the family was together. He was also the polite one and the one that they all agreed to be the most loyal and family-oriented.

He didn't say much, but his eyes would scan the room for Penelope often. When Penelope also noticed this, her cheeks would turn a light shade of pink. She would often avert her eyes, but Amanda saw the few instances where her eyes would meet his. There was a current of electricity in the air. Amanda could feel the effects of it from across the room. Was that what she and Romeo seemed like to others?

Amanda's brother had disappeared along with Lilith, but Amanda knew that it wasn't over. She could feel her brother breathing down her back. She would catch herself looking around, feeling like someone was watching her. Whether he was close enough to see her or he used his magic, she knew her brother was watching. She had often spoken to Penelope about it, and the other woman had decided to increase the frequency of Amanda's magic lessons because of it.

She guessed the other woman could feel the anxiety building as well. Something was going to happen, and it was going to be big. She knew her brother would have something to do with it, would probably be the whole reason behind whatever chaos would ensue. The only problem was they didn't know what exactly to expect from him. He was sneaky and conniving.

Amanda and Penelope were Radiants; two out of the four most powerful witches in the world. Soon, the news would be out, and the other two Radiants would meet up with them. They were sure of it. Amanda was so excited to meet the Fire Radiant and the Water Radiant.

She was sitting alone on the porch when Penelope made her way over. Penelope was petite and one of the most stunningly beautiful people Amanda had ever seen. She seemed so regal in her posture and movements. But she never seemed to hold herself above others.

Amanda had seen her in the dirt playing marbles with some of the kids just the day before. Her white shirt had been brown by the time she stood up. The funniest part was watching her play the childhood game as her tongue stuck from the corner of her mouth. She had an amazing laugh. Her cheeks had been tinged pink, and her long blond hair had been matted at the ends where it trailed the dirt while she crawled around on her knees.

Penelope had relayed to Amanda the nature of her childhood, or lack thereof. Her father had never allowed Penelope to play with other children, and she often wasn't allowed outside. In the beginning, her mother would sneak her out or she would fight with Penelope's father until he would finally give in and let her go out. Her mother very rarely lost an argument with anyone, including her father. Penelope thought it was in part because he was so scared of her. That was the reason for the poison he'd used to kill her. What a coward.

The servants had told Penelope what happened.
They had said her father wanted to take her mother
breakfast in bed, and he had them prepare the meal.
They figured he must have added the poison on his way
up the stairs, because her mother was gone the very
next day. Their suspicions about the circumstances
grew when he always seemed to be with Penelope's
adopted sister, who was just a few years older than
herself. She was proved correct when she snuck
downstairs in the middle of the night. Lilith leaned over
a desk with her father behind her. It was an image that
was scalded into Penelope's brain. The worst part was
the conversation afterward, where the both of them had
clarified their plot to kill her mother.

Two of the servants loyal to her mother were
standing in the doorway across from her. One of them
had grabbed her and covered her mouth as they took her
through a hidden doorway back to her room. They had
shushed her and stroked her hair. They had tried
reassuring her everything would be okay. They told her
that they would help to protect her, and they wouldn't
let anything happen to her. That was the last time she
ever saw them. A new housekeeper and butler started
the very next day. From that point on, she had stayed
hidden from everyone, especially her father and Lilith.
She knew that her mother had given her powers to her,
and she studied on how to use them, but never had the
nerve to try anything out.

"Hey, Penelope. What's going on?"

"I came to talk. I wanted to talk to you before, but
we needed to be alone."

"Okay." Amanda instantly began to feel worried. What did Penelope not want to say in front of the others?

"Well, you know there are two other Radiants, and we will probably be meeting them anytime now."

"Yes. It is exciting to meet new people, especially ones who will have the same powers as we do."

"Yes, but I don't think you know the full extent of your situation."

"What do you mean?"

"Your power is on the line, Amanda." Penelope looked sad for a moment.

"Well, I mean, I know that. Look, I know I have just recently found out that all of this stuff is even real, and I am just now coming into my full blown powers, but I can learn fast." Would they take her powers from her? Could they do that? She knew black magic could, but would the other Radiants resort to that?

"That is not what I am talking about, Amanda."

"Then what are you talking about?" A chill ran down Amanda's spine. Were there more stories; more secrets?

If you enjoyed this sample then look for **Romeo Alpha: A BBW Paranormal Shifter Romance - Book 2.**

Here is a preview of **another story** you may also enjoy:

Devil's Advocate: A BBW MC New Adult Romance Series - Book 2 by Carla Coxwell

KRISTIE LOOKED at herself in the mirror, doing a last-minute touch up before she walked out into her party. Her mother and Lionel had rented out her favorite place to eat, and the guests milled around outside, talking in low tones. She was ten minutes late for her own party. It all boiled down to one guest she was dreading to see.

Her graduation had gone off without a hitch, and her heart had raced with excitement the entire time. This was what she had been working so hard for. It had been a long journey, but she had done it. Kristie couldn't believe that she was now an English graduate.

The last semester had been touch and go. After a holiday filled with nothing but tense moments and one stressful event after another, Kristie had come back to her dorm in a state of mental anguish. Even though she had a new boyfriend, she still couldn't help but think about Gray.

Always Gray. The final semester, Gray had kept floating into her mind. How could she feel this way about her own cousin? Upon meeting her mother's new husband, she had also met his nephew, Gray. Her connection with Gray had been immediate. She had felt something with him that she had never felt before. And he had felt it as well.

The two of them had slept together twice and fooled around once. Kristie had wanted to be with him and pushed aside any negativity that could be in their way.

She had wanted to make it work, ignoring their vast differences, since Gray was the leader of a motorcycle gang.

But ultimately, their lives were too different. Armand, a member of Gray's gang, the Devil's Advocates, had accidently killed someone in an illegal street race. Officer John, a cop Kristie had briefly dated, had wanted to arrest Gray, who had skipped town once he had gotten wind of the arrest. The two of them had parted on bad terms.

But now, summer was upon them. In a twist of fate, Kristie had found comfort in Armand. In Gray's absence, she had grown fond of him and the two of them had been dating steadily since she had gone back to college. The long distance had been hard, but Armand would come up to visit whenever he could.

A sudden knock at the door jarred Kristie from her walk down memory lane.

"Kristie? It's Kass."

Kristie let out a sigh of relief and opened the door, letting her friend in. Kass had fallen hard for Rick, Gray's second in command at the Devil's Advocates, and the two of them were now engaged. Her engagement ring sparkled under the dim lighting of the bathroom. They had barely been dating for six months. Kristie thought it was too whirlwind for her liking, but Kass only looked happy when she was around Rick.

"Hey, you're taking forever. You look great. What's the hold up?"

Gray and Armand being in the same room together. "Just nervous. A lot of people. Not a huge fan of crowds."

Kass nodded as if she understood, even though Kristie knew she was a social butterfly. "Well, it's all people who are thrilled with you. Even your cousin showed up. I haven't seen him since he skipped town when everyone saw John gunning after him."

Kristie went to run her fingers through her hair, but at the last moment remembered it was up in a fancy bun. "Yeah, well, John took a leave of absence after that mess."

There were rumors that the leave of absence was forced because John had gone after Gray with no true evidence. Kristie didn't know. She tried not to think about the whole thing.

"So come on! Armand is waiting, too."

Kristie gave one final glance in the mirror, knowing that she couldn't put it off any longer. It was time. She followed Kass out of the bathroom and down the hallway leading to the main floor of the restaurant. Her mother had invited what felt like half the town because she was so excited. Kristie didn't see them as she stepped out onto the main floor. Her eyes scanned for one person and one person only.

Her mother and Lionel swarmed her first, congratulating her. Lionel would never replace her father, but she knew her mom was happy with him. He was a hard-working man, gentle and kind, and Kristie had warmed up to him the last few months.

Her mother was the same as always. Overly excited, trying to smooth out part of Kristie's dress as she shielded her from the crowd.

"A little snug," she commented quickly before moving to announce her to everyone.

Kristie felt her face flush. The last thing she wanted to hear was something from her mom about her weight. The tiny comments here and there, reminding Kristie that she wasn't super model thin, always stuck underneath her skin like tiny needles.

Everyone swarmed around her, people she knew and some she had never seen in her life. They shook her hand and asked a few questions. *Must be proud of yourself, right? Are you going to be an English teacher? I personally wouldn't have gone to college for English, but I'm glad you found your niche. Settling down after this, I presume?* All the comments made her skin itch.

In the midst of all of this, Armand found her. People tended to give her boyfriend a wide berth. He was burly and bulky. Kristie could imagine him being a gladiator back in the olden days, swinging a sword around and taking people down. But in this day and age, he was just a biker.

Armand had dressed up a little today for her. His clothes were faded and clearly old, but the effort counted for something. She smiled when she saw him, and her heart skipped a beat. Almost everyone she knew disapproved of her dating Armand. Even she didn't understand the connection that she felt with him. They were part of different worlds, like she and Gray had been, but there was one less obstacle with him – he wasn't her cousin.

Besides, many times, late at night, Kristie told herself that she wouldn't ever settle down with Armand. *He works for where I am in my life right now and nothing more.* But Armand had no idea she thought such things.

Her thoughts were cut off by Armand pulling her into a bear hug, pressing his lips against hers. Kristie kissed back and quickly pulled away, always too shy to show too much affection in public. Armand pulled away but kept his arm wrapped around her waist. There was something different in the way that he was holding her. She knew why – Gray. Everything boiled down to Gray.

Almost as if Kristie thinking about him had conjured him up, the crowd parted and Gray stepped forward.

If you enjoyed this sample then look for **Devil's Advocate: A BBW MC New Adult Romance Series - Book 2 by Carla Coxwell**.

Other Books by Darla Dunbar

- The Romeo Alpha BBW Paranormal Shifter Romance Series (This series precedes the "Romeo Alpha Blood Lines Romance Series")

- The Alpha Feud BBW Paranormal Shifter Romance Series

- The Alpha Packed BBW Paranormal Shifter Romance Series

- The Daemon Paranormal Romance Chronicles

- The Mind Talker Paranormal Romance Series

- The Leather Satchel Paranormal Romance Series

Get the latest update on new releases from the author at:

https://darladunbar.com/newsletter/

About the Author - Darla Dunbar

Darla has been interested in paranormal romance since she was a teenager in high school. It was then that she discovered she could fulfill her fantasies through her writing.

Observing people and human behavior in the area of romance has always been one of her favorite pastimes. Combining that with an overactive imagination is a sure fire way of coming up with interesting themes.

Connect with Darla Dunbar

I really appreciate you reading my book! Here are my social media coordinates:

Friend me on Facebook:
https://www.facebook.com/darladunbar/

Follow me on Twitter: https://twitter.com/DarlDunbar

Check me out on Goodreads:
https://www.goodreads.com/author/show/8425857.Darl a_Dunbar

Subscribe to my newsletter:
https://darladunbar.com/newsletter/

Visit my website: https://darladunbar.com/

www.ingramcontent.com/pod-product-compliance
Lightning Source LLC
Chambersburg PA
CBHW030755200726

48288CB00004B/1190